Midnight's Kiss

Indulgences Series - Book Ten

By Authors:

Victoria Zak & D.L. Roan

Copyright

Midnight's Kiss, Indulgence Series – Book 10

Victoria Zak

Copyright © Victoria Zak, 2016

Edited by: Violetta Rand

Cover by: JAB Designs

ISBN-13: 978-1-942516-17-0

Contents

Dear Reader,

Welcome to **Midnight's Kiss,** one of the twelve books in the *Indulgences* series where twelve authors offer the stories of people who came to Indulgences Resort to live out their fantasy. It's not just a beautiful place, but also, as you will find, has magical secrets. Each fantasy will come to life, taking guests on an adventure that could change the rest of their lives.

Although each book is a standalone, I suggest that you start by reading *Indulgences, The Prequel* so you can meet the staff of Indulgences Resort. You'll see some these characters in every story.

Indulgences, The Prequel by Hildie McQueen

Hearts Adrift by C. Knight - a second chance at true love for childhood sweethearts lost in the past, but hopeful for the future. Heat level 3

A Game of Hearts by Tigris Eden - best friends since childhood, Zori and Matteo traveled to Paradise and try their hand at A Game of Hearts. Heat level 5

Watching Mia by Olivia Gaines - a sexy bartender serves as a catalyst to put a spark back into a struggling marriage, Heat level 3

Yours for the Weekend by Lana Williams - a millionaire businessman hires a date for his friend's wedding, only to realize a weekend with the sexy grad student won't be enough. Heat level 3.5

Cowboy in Paradise by Hildie McQueen - years after losing the love of his life, a cowboy may find it again in Paradise. Heat level 3+

Undertones by Xyla Turner - two scarred strangers meet to find a fantasy that only the other can fulfill. Heat level 4

Summer in Paradise by J.D. Monroe - on the job in an island paradise, two old high school friends get a second chance at true love. Heat level 3

Double Jeopardy by KaLyn Cooper - saving the lives of a billionaire and his wife gives their bodyguards a second chance at love. Heat level 3+

Take Me Away by Allie K. Adams - sometimes your worst enemy is your greatest ally. Heat level 3

Midnight's Kiss by Victoria Zak/D.L. Roan – an unexpected fantasy ignites a love that lasts forever. Heat level 4

So Great a Love by T.M. Cromer - an estranged couple reunited in Paradise will either rekindle their passion or be forced to move on from what could be the love of a lifetime. Heat level 3

Hired Heart by Elizabeth Rose - a Scrooge of a businessman and his sexy coworker end up in Paradise where business takes a backseat to pleasure. Heat level 3

Join the Facebook group to get in on the fun! Giveaways, free books, prizes, and sharing by best-selling authors.

https://www.facebook.com/groups/719439014873659/

CHAPTER
One

"Antonio, I understand how you feel, but—*Sì*. Of course. I'll be there. *Arrivederci*."

"*Cazzo!*" Dario Dicola slammed his cellphone down on his desk.

Irritated, he ran his hands through his dark hair with a heavy sigh. When he'd decided to follow-up on the multi-million-dollar business proposal he'd sent to Antonio to build a lavish condo community on Antonio's resort island, the last thing he expected was a last-minute trip to Panama. Even though his investment partner, Cassandra, had warned him that Antonio stood firm on his refusal to further develop the eco-friendly paradise, Dario refused to take no for an answer. Antonio simply hadn't been approached by the right investor.

Leaning back in his leather office chair with his hands behind his head, he stared up at the ceiling and took a deep breath, releasing some of the tension caused by his clipped conversation with Antonio. Failure wasn't an option. If Antonio insisted he come to the island in person, then that's where he was going, but make no mistake, this deal was going to go through.

He was the most successful real estate developer in Milan, owning four hundred retail and office buildings, over one hundred apartment complexes, and four, upscale hotels, he knew success, and intended to add Aragon Island to his long list of accomplishments. After seeing pictures and videos of the Indulgence Resort, the lush island beckoned him, so much so, it had taken priority over all other projects.

However, wasting valuable business time traveling to the island wasn't the ideal situation, but he wanted this deal. So, when Antonio made a compromise, Dario accepted his challenge. Come to the resort and experience the beauty and mystery of the island first-hand. If, after one week, his fantasy wasn't fulfilled, Antonio would sit down with him and consider his offer. It was further than any investor had ever gotten with Antonio. With that thought, a sly grin spread across his lips.

What Antonio didn't realize was Dario already had the upper hand—he didn't have a fantasy. He was living the billionaire dream—money, beautiful women, and traveling world-class on private jets. This deal was more than business, now. Antonio had made it personal. The challenge had been accepted. He'd go to the resort, talk with Antonio face-to-face, and close the deal.

Dario sat up and rolled his chair closer to his desk. He picked up the headset and pressed the red blinking light on his office phone, calling his longtime assistant.

Buongiorno, you have reached Gina…

Aggravated by the recorded voice on the other end of the phone, Dario threw the receiver down. *Where is she?*

"Buongiorno, Mr. Dicola."

Gina breezed through his office door, beaming like one of his many lovers the morning after a long, hot night of sex, with her arms full of items from her routine Monday morning duties. Dario narrowed his eyes. As far as how good of a morning it was, that was yet to be determined.

Gina unloaded the items, placing his morning coffee on his desk as she balanced department store bags in her other hand. Her purse strap slipped, causing her to almost spill coffee on the dry-cleaning.

Dario stood and then walked out from behind his desk. "You should delegate some of your workload to other people." He took the bags, sneaking a peek inside. Three lacy, baby doll lingerie sets with matching G-strings stared up at him. He grumbled inside a little, knowing he'd never get to enjoy the gifts.

Gina sashayed to the closet, her hips sensuously swaying in her pinstriped, knee-length skirt and matching suit jacket. Leaning against his desk, Dario watched her reach into the closet and hang up his dry-cleaning.

Gina was one of the first employees he'd hired when he opened his Milan headquarters years ago. She was extremely valuable to his company, which made her one-hundred-percent off limits. When it came to his empire, it was strictly business. He didn't have time for frivolous lawsuits that would tarnish his company's good name because he couldn't keep it in his pants. No, there was a definitive line between business and pleasure.

"Do you actually think anyone in this office can get your coffee exactly the way you like it?" she asked, her lips curled into a knowing smile as she made her way back to the desk. "And look this good doing it?"

"You do have a point." *Busted.* He gave her a sly grin. Off limits or not, her legs could make a blind man blush.

Gina grabbed the bags and pulled out the lingerie, one item at a time. "Just like you said, one in purple." She held the lacy material up. "One in red." She laid each one over her shoulder as she emptied the bag. "And one in green."

"Yeah, about that." Dario scrubbed his chin as Gina arched her brow. "I'm going to need you to clear my schedule for the rest of the week."

Gina's good mood immediately vanished, signified by a frustrated sigh and eye roll.

Dario pushed off the desk and walked back behind it, straightening a stack of papers. His already foul mood soured even further. Not only was he canceling important business meetings, he was clearing his personal schedule. Tiffany—Tuesday night, Maria—Wednesday, and what was the redhead's name? Ah yes, Chanel. One night was never enough with her.

"Gina." He sighed. "I need you to move everything back a week except for the Bernardo project." The one investor he couldn't reschedule was Dino Bernardo. With him in route, there was no time to cancel. Construction on the luxury villas downtown started in less than a week and he needed Gina's charm to keep his guest occupied until he returned. "And get Sal to ready the jet. I want to leave in an hour."

"An hour?" Gina blurted, "I know I can work magic, but one hour to cancel and move appointments and pack, you're asking for a miracle."

"No. Gina, I need you to stay here and entertain Mr. Bernardo until I return next Monday."

"Mr. Bernardo? *The* Mr. Bernardo?" Gina asked, her mouth agape in shock.

"Yes," Dario confirmed as he stuffed folders from his desk into his briefcase. "Dino loves to wine and dine beautiful women. You should have no problem keeping him occupied."

"But you never travel alone."

"I know, but I must take this trip." He shoved another file into his briefcase. "If everything falls into place, I'll be back in a week with a little piece of paradise to add to my empire."

Gina's incredulous scowl relaxed into a reluctant pout. "Fine. But what am I supposed to do with these?" Gina held up the lacy red lingerie.

"You keep them." He smiled wickedly. "I'm sure I'm not the only one who could appreciate them."

"Great, I'll add it to my collection." She tossed the lingerie in the bag. "Now I have a complete set in every color."

Gina turned on her heels to leave, but Dario caught her in time before she left. "One more thing, double-book my personal schedule next week. Add an extra day with Chanel."

"In all my years working for you I've never seen you drop everything at a moment's notice. Where are you going?"

Dario peered up from his bag, his deep thoughts already weighing on his resolve. "Panama."

Two cocktails into his twelve-hour flight, Dario pulled his briefcase into his lap. While he dreaded the idle time, the long flight gave him ample opportunity to read through the contract for Aragon Island, making sure there were no loopholes. He popped open the case and thumbed through the files he'd packed. As he reached the end of the stack, his forehead creased. Where was the Indulgence folder? He remembered straightening the stack while back at his office. Dammit, he'd left it on his desk.

Praying he'd overlooked the documents, he searched again—the contract wasn't there. Quickly, he checked his Rolex. Gina should still be at the office. He tugged his cell out of his breast pocket and checked for service. *None*! He growled in frustration—just his luck.

He tossed the phone on the seat next to him. Ten more hours sky-bound with an idle mind, insanity was assured. Normally, Gina accompanied him on business trips, briefing him on their current destination and dealings. What was he going to do now?

Dario looked out of the window, scrubbing his closely shaven jaw. It was the stillness that he hated the most. With no distractions, his inner demons came out to play, tormenting and poking their icy fingers into an empty void that sat where his heart used to be. No amount of possessions could fill the depth—he'd tried. Over the years, he'd found creative ways to ignore it but it never truly relented.

He'd grown up watching his father struggle to keep the family clothed and fed, but many times he'd gone to school with a rumbling belly. As he grew older, he found his own ways to help put food on the table, even stealing it when he had to. One day, his neighbor, who was a local police officer, caught him stuffing a loaf of bread in his coat. He'd never forget the disappointment in his papa's eyes.

That night, his father sat him down and instilled the value of an honest living and how important it was to stay in school so he *could* have a better life. *Intelligence is power,* he'd said. From that moment on, he'd lived and breathed school. He took extra classes and worked nights at the local restaurant bussing tables, where he met a local businessman who took him under his wing, helped him get into college and introduced him to the lavish world of investment development.

Even in his success, he never lost that little boy inside who craved his father's approval and respect. Before he'd made his first million, he'd paid off his parents' debts and bought them a new house in the country. He even bought his papa the classic roadster he'd always dreamed of driving one day. Dario grinned at the memory of the surprise on the old man's face when he'd handed over the keys. He'd never looked more young and alive than he did that day. His papa was his hero. He'd been a good, strong man, the best father a kid could have, until his mother died. Her death crushed them all, but in a sense, his papa had died with her.

Dario looked up through the clouds, the warm sunlight filtering through the window and soothing some of the rawness he still felt when he thought about his parents. Up here, away from all the distractions, he could feel their presence. He said a silent prayer, letting them know how much he missed them and that he wished he'd spent more time with them when he'd had the chance. But even as he said the words, he knew he wouldn't have changed anything. He would never regret giving his parents the life they'd deserved, if even only for a short while. Now, that life served as his constant reminder to remain an island unto himself, driven by success instead of the fleeting and ultimately destructive entanglements of emotional commitment.

He'd worked hard, building his company from the ground up, and nothing would jeopardize his success—not even a woman. He had everything he needed, or could ever want for that matter. Didn't he?

The plane hit a patch of turbulence, giving him a mental shake from his morose thoughts. This was why he hated these long trips. Downing the rest of his cocktail, he reclined back in his seat and stuffed earbuds in his ears. He pressed the button on the armrest and raised the volume until light classical music drowned out the sound of his doubts.

As soon as he closed his eyes and felt himself drifting off to sleep, he was wakened by his personal flight attendant. Frustrated, he sat up, pulling the earbuds from his ears.

11

"Mr. Dicola, we're getting ready to land."

What? He hadn't slept through the flight—had he? He scrubbed his hands over his face, and then reached into his pocket for his phone to check the time. *Nine-eighteen A.M.* Seven hours ahead of Milan time and his morning had started all over again.

As the jet descended, Dario watched out the window. It looked as if Sal was flying straight into the Amazon, not a single sign of an airport or tarmac in sight. Sending up a silent Hail Mary, he white-knuckled the arm rest and closed his eyes as the plane thrusted forward into the lush jungle greenery.

"Sal!" Dario bit out through clenched teeth. He wasn't usually one to sweat rough landings, but holy hell!

With an abrupt jerk, the jet screeched to a stop. Slowly, he opened his eyes as the tarmac magically appeared. Blessed Virgin, he exhaled, thankful Sal hadn't crashed into the tropical abyss—Tarzan he was not. When Antonio had said his resort was secluded, he wasn't lying.

"Sir," Sal's unsteady voice sounded through the cabin intercom. "Welcome to Panama."

Apparently, he wasn't the only one shaken. Dario released a relieved breath and reigned in his rattled nerves. He stood and stretched his stiff muscles. The quicker he was off this damn plane, the better. Grabbing his satchel and phone, he quickly made his way to the front, anxious to stand on solid ground.

He stepped off the plane into the bright tropical oasis. A warm salty breeze blew over him like a lover's kiss and something stirred inside him. Perhaps it was the excitement of the deal he'd coveted for so long, or the nap he'd taken on the flight that gave him a sense of eager anticipation for what awaited.

Be careful what you wish for.

Antonio's words ghosted through his thoughts, but he laughed the warning away. As charming and invigorating as the island may be, he didn't have a fantasy Antonio could use to sway him from the reason he was there. Slipping on his polarized sunglasses, Dario descended the stairs with renewed certainty. Antonio and a silver-haired woman waited by a convertible Jeep with painted palm fronds and the Indulgences logo on the side—his ride to the resort no doubt. Clearing his throat and mentally summoning his A-game, he was ready to impress and conquer.

"*Buongiorno*," he said with a smile, extending a confident hand to greet his future business partner.

CHAPTER
Two

Kenderly turned her face into the warm breeze as it swept through the open shuttle window, breathing in the change she felt coursing all around her as she and Antonio began their twenty-minute ride to meet their next guest at Aragon Island's private airport. Only a few weeks had passed since a hurricane had assaulted their remote paradise. The cutting winds and driving rain had ravaged the lush green landscape for days. Thankfully, except for a handful of dedicated staff, the guests had been evacuated in plenty of time. The resort itself had sustained very little damage.

Unwilling to leave, she and Antonio had remained on the island, safe in the knowledge that Antonio had built the resort with such forces of nature in mind. When the storm passed and they ventured outside to survey the damage, she'd been reminded of just how fragile life was. Mankind often forgot how powerful Mother Nature could be. Weeks later, the island still bore the marks of her wrath, but Kenderly wasn't worried. Nature had a way about her that always gave back more than she took.

It wasn't the physical changes from the storm that caught her notice so much as the changes in the energy that floated on the wind that morning. On their way to greet Antonio's unexpected guest, she could sense a shift coming. More often than not, when a guest arrived, her gifts would allow her a sneak peek into their personalities, their innermost fantasies. She couldn't help but think the sudden change in energy was a prelude to this particular arrival.

Antonio's previous lover, Cassandra, had been hounding him for months to sell a portion of their island to her group of fortune-hungry investors, one of whom—the most wealthy and aggressive—was Dario Dicola, a billionaire who apparently didn't take no for an answer.

Despite being a hot-blooded Latino, Antonio wasn't one to lose his temper often. But it had taken her two hours to sooth his ruffled feathers after taking Mr. Dicola's call. She'd almost felt sorry for Cassandra when Antonio called her out for giving the Italian investor his private number. When she'd heard that Antonio had invited Dario to the island, and even agreed to meet with him once his stay had concluded, she'd been shocked to say the least. Antonio had sworn to never sell even the smallest piece of their paradise.

"Don't worry, Love." Sitting beside her, Antonio kissed her palm. "When this week is over, Mr. Dicola will understand the magic our paradise holds. And when he does, it will finally put an end to his and Cassandra's persistent pressuring to develop Aragon Island into something it's not."

Kenderly thought to argue with him, but held her tongue, smiling when she met his reassuring gaze. "I hope you're right, darling." She had faith in Antonio's judgment, and in their island, but she also knew not to ignore the feelings that stirred inside her. Something was about to change.

The custom-made shuttle bounced over a few bumps in the unpaved road that provided the only access from the resort to the airport. They'd had it resurfaced since the storm, but the extra traffic during the cleanup had left it less than pristine for their guests. Kenderly made a mental note to ask Mario to inform the maintenance crew, then chuckled when she heard Antonio already tapping out a message.

"Tell Mario it's not the same without him," she said.

Indulgence's event coordinator, Mario, was an intricate part of their lives on the island and completely irreplaceable. On any other day, he would be sitting across from them dressed in one of his brightly colored island shirts, preening his shoulder-length hair before meeting their guests. An unfortunate accident that morning had sent him into a panicked frenzy. Apparently, when the salon was restocked after the storm, someone had mixed up the hair dye toners. Fuchsia was *not* his color.

"I don't see what the problem is," Antonio remarked as he dropped his phone back into the breast pocket of his navy blazer. "Nothing could be worse than that hideous lime he loves so much."

"Stop picking on the man," Kenderly playfully admonished. "You can't fault him for wanting to look nice for our guests. First impressions are important."

Antonio harrumphed, but she could tell by the difficulty he had hiding his grin that he was more amused than agitated by Mario's absence.

"Speaking of nice." Antonio reached up to finger a lock of her hair. "Have I told you how ravishing you look this morning?"

She turned her face into his palm and kissed his wrist. "Yes, but I never tire of hearing it." Antonio considered her a moment, the corners of his mouth curling up into a hungry smile she knew all too well. "Oh, no." She withdrew from him with a playful laugh. "We can't be late to meet your special guest. Besides, it took Catalina an hour to weave this intricate pattern," she said, running her hand over the long silver braid hanging over her shoulder. "Five minutes with you and I'll look like an island savage."

"Sounds exotic," Antonio said with a salacious wink. "How is Catalina?" he asked when it became clear she wasn't giving in to his seductive objective. "I regret that I haven't had the time to catch up with her or the other staff since the storm."

"She's worked her fingers to the bone since returning from the mainland to check on her family." As head of the housekeeping staff, Catalina was so much more than a maid. Kenderly had come to love her as a friend, as well as depend on her to keep the resort gleaming for their guests. "I do worry she's overdoing it, though. She takes so little time for herself."

"Maybe, on the next off week, we should insist that she does," Antonio suggested. "I'm sure she would appreciate the extra time with her family."

That's what Kenderly was afraid of. Catalina had sacrificed everything to support her large family. She could see the toll the hard work was taking on her. Catalina was a young, vibrant woman. Though she rarely complained, her friend needed to indulge in her own fantasies for once. "I'll speak with her again," Kenderly said with a doubtful sigh as the shuttle pulled onto the tarmac. Maybe she needed to get creative. Weaving fantasies is what the island was about, after all.

The shuttle pulled up to the plane just as the door opened. Antonio took her hand and helped her out, the bright island sun hot and high in the sky. When Mr. Dicola appeared at the top of the stairs, Kenderly drew in a shuddering breath.

"What's wrong?" Antonio asked.

Kenderly shook her head, careful to hold her welcoming smile. Mr. Dicola was every bit the stylish, handsome mogul his profile portrayed, much taller than she'd imagined, ducking to clear the doorway before he descended to greet them. What struck her the most was not his charming smile or his confident stature, but the utter loneliness she sensed hiding behind them.

"Mr. Dicola." Antonio stretched out his hand. "Welcome to Indulgence. I trust you had a nice flight."

"A long flight to be exact, but other than the landing, uneventful."

"Glad to hear it," Antonio quipped and turned to Kenderly. "May I introduce my partner in business and in love, Kenderly. Kenderly, this is Mr. Dicola, the investor Cassandra has mentioned on occasion."

"Dario," he insisted, bending over her hand to bestow a disarming kiss. "And I do hope Cassandra has mentioned me more than occasionally," he said, turning his attention back to Antonio. "Although, that would explain why I'm here, instead of in my office in Milan closing a deal to buy a piece of this paradise."

"We don't have a deal yet," Antonio politely reminded him. "Only an agreement to talk once you've completed your stay here."

Kenderly watched and listened on their ride back to the resort, intrigued by Dario's effortless success at hiding his inner feelings. His smile was as easy as the breeze. His eyes, though hidden behind a fashionable pair of sunglasses, crinkled in the corners with his careless laugh, and no doubt held the same heat that ran through his Mediterranean blood. He wasn't a dark man inside, she decided fairly early in their conversation, but there was definitely more to him than met the eye.

The jeep pulled up to the portico in front of the resort and Kenderly accepted Dario's hand to help her out.

"Thank you," she said with a polite nod as she preceded them up the stairs into the lobby.

"Come." Antonio nodded toward the patio beyond the wall of glass that framed the back of the resort, overlooking the eastern island shoreline. "We'll enjoy a refreshing drink by the pool while Kenderly consults with you about your stay."

"Consult?" Dario asked when they were seated around one of the marble tables beside the pool. "I wasn't aware that a tropical vacation required a consultation."

"Please, forgive me," Antonio offered. "We've done things a bit out of order it seems. We normally have our guests complete an extensive questionnaire before their arrival so that we might better facilitate their wishes and fantasies."

"Ah, yes. Fantasy." Dario chuckled. "Oh, my fantasies are quite simple I assure you. In fact," he glanced around the poolside, and then up toward the tiki bar, pulling his sunglasses down to peer over the rim. "If she's willing, we could wrap this up in a single night. No need to drag it out for an entire week."

Kenderly looked over her shoulder to see who he was referring to, frowning when Catalina turned around with a drink tray in her hands. She walked toward them. What was she doing working the bar?

"I'm afraid it's not quite that simple." Antonio smiled at Cat when she approached, but neither of them questioned her reasoning for being there as she set their drinks on the table, sweet vermouth for her, and Antonio's customary Cognac.

"I hope you don't mind." Antonio nodded to the last glass in Cat's hand. "I took the liberty of asking Cassandra about your drink of choice."

Dario reached for the glass of fine Italian wine as Cat took a step forward to hand it to him. Their hands collided. The glass slipped from her fingers. In slow motion, Kenderly watched as the wine sloshed out of the tumbling glass and onto the sleeve of Dario's tailored suit jacket, the sound of shattering glass the final sonata in their clumsy, symphonic introduction.

"Oh, my gosh! I'm so sorry!" Cat immediately dropped to the deck and began picking up the larger shards of glass, but Dario reached down to stop her.

Cat rose to her feet and froze, her gaze locked with Dario's. Kenderly felt the moment it happened. Their connection coursed through her veins as if she'd felt it herself. For a split second, the overwhelming loneliness she'd sensed in Dario was eclipsed by a glimpse of a new fantasy. Cat's fantasy.

"It's no problem at all." Dario pulled a handkerchief from his breast pocket, but instead of whisking it over his sleeve, he wiped the drops of wine from Cat's arm. When he reached her hand, he pulled it to his lips and kissed the burgundy drops from her knuckles.

Cat snatched her hand away, glancing nervously between Dario and Antonio. "My apologies," she said. "I'll pay for—"

"You'll do no such thing," Dario insisted.

Sensing Cat's distress, Kenderly rushed to ease her fears. "Catalina, this is Dario Dicola, our honored guest for the week. Dario, this is our hospitality manager, Catalina. We gave our staff some extra time on the mainland to see to the wellbeing of their families after the storm, and Cat is filling in at the bar today."

"It's a pleasure," Dario said with all the charm of a devilish prince.

Cat blushed. "I am truly sorry about your—"

"Catalina, can you please ask Mario to escort Mr. Dicola to his cabana," Kenderly interjected. "I believe his luggage should be there by now and I'm sure he'd like a moment to freshen up."

Catalina nodded, gave Dario one last apologetic glance, then scurried off.

"We can finish the consultation after you've changed and had a moment to rest," Antonio suggested.

"There's no need to bother with the usual formalities, darling." Confident in her intuition, Kenderly gave Dario a polite smile before she took a sip of her drink and relaxed against the back of her chair. "I believe we already have everything we need to make Dario's stay at Indulgence a memorable one indeed."

CHAPTER
Three

Cat cursed as she rushed through the foyer toward the salon to find Mario, crashing into Kenderly and Antonio's personal maid as she rounded the corner into the hallway. *Damn-damn-damn!*

"Oh, *Dios mio!*" Rosa's hand flew to her chest as the tall stack of folded beach towels she was carrying toppled to the polished marble floor.

"Rosa! I'm so sorry!" Cat knelt and scooped them up, but the damage was done, most of them now needing to be refolded. "I don't know what's wrong with me!" Everything she'd touched since waking up that morning had either ended up on the floor or spilled on their guests.

"I tell you again, *gatita*," Rosa admonished. "You need to slow down."

Cat blew out a breath, brushing away the stray tendrils of hair that had come loose from her ponytail. "Rosa, please. Not now. I have to find Mario."

"Too much work and no play, this is no good. Kittens, they are meant to play once in a while."

Cat scooped up the last remaining towel and tossed it into Rosa's arms before she took off down the hallway again.

"*Gatita!*" Rosa called out to her in a sing-song voice. Cat slid to a stop and turned back to her. "Mario is this way. I saw him in his office on my way to the laundry."

Cat reversed course, stopping to give Rosa a peck on the cheek. "*Gracias!*"

"Slow down!" Rosa shouted after her as she rounded the corner and sprinted to the other end of the resort, stopping short when she came to Mario's open office door to find him still on the phone.

"Yes, two o'clock is perfect. The guests will arrive at the helipad at one-thirty, so have the limousine waiting. *Gracias.*"

"Antonio needs you poolside." Catalina rushed over and grabbed Mario's hand.

He pulled her to a stop when she tried to drag him out of the office.

"I need to make one last call," he argued.

"This can't wait," Cat insisted. "Antonio's VIP is..." *Breathtaking.* She shook the memory of Dario's hypnotic stare and captivating smile from her head. *Don't go there, Cat.* "He's, uh, well, he's—"

"He's what?" Mario asked, concern marring his usual carefree countenance. "What's got your spandex in a twist, honey? Did he do something inappropriate? I'll kill him!"

"No! Nothing like that." *Oh, man.* Maybe she needed to take Kenderly up on her advice and take some time off.

She'd had many guests flirt with her since first coming to work for Antonio and Kenderly, but none of them as potently charming as Mr. Dicola. Fraternizing with the guests wasn't strictly forbidden, but she had no room in her life for indulgence and fantasy, short-term or otherwise.

"He's out by the pool with Antonio and Kenderly. I may have spilled a three hundred-dollar glass of wine on his four thousand-dollar suit." She cringed as the words left her lips. "And then I offered to pay for his dry cleaning—oh God, I'm so fired." *Stains like that don't come out!* "I haven't waited tables since I came to the island. I should have never offered to take Soraya's shift."

"Shh." Mario took her by the elbow and walked her out of his office toward the pool. "No one's getting fired, honey, least of all, *you*. It was an accident, yes?"

Cat nodded.

"Antonio and Kenderly will understand."

Cat swallowed. She hoped so. She and Kenderly had become friends over the last year, but she was still her boss. "Kenderly asked me to come find you to show Mr. Dicola to his cabana so he can change."

Mario stopped short when they reached the entrance to the pool. "Oh, honey. Is that him?" He dipped his head to peer over the rim of his sunglasses at Mr. Dicola relaxing by the pool. Cat's stomach fluttered at the sight of him. His coat draped over his knee, he was sprawled out in his seat, his shirt unbuttoned and the wine-stained sleeves rolled up to show his sinewy, tanned forearms.

"No wonder you're walking funny," Mario said with a chuckle.

Cat glanced down at her feet, then gave Mario a playful shove. "I am not."

"Stand right here," he said and pushed his sunglasses back up onto his nose. "I'll try to get him to take off his shirt before we head down to the cabana."

"Don't you dare!" Cat said with a gasp. "If you're going to try anything, try to keep him from getting me fired."

"Have it your way." Mario waved her off as he pushed through the doors.

She watched anxiously until they left the patio before she returned to the bar. If she was lucky, she'd get through the rest of her shift without spilling any more drinks, and the rest of her life without seeing Mr. Dicola again.

The next morning, Cat sat downstairs in the resort's formal dining room eating a piece of toast to calm her queasy stomach before she headed to Kenderly's office. The night had been long and restless with the thought of losing her job. In addition to her disappointment in letting Kenderly down, she was so close to reaching the end of her two-year contract. She couldn't afford to lose this job, especially over a klutzy move like spilling drinks. Having woken that morning to an urgent email from Kenderly requesting an unscheduled meeting, she got the feeling that was exactly what was about to happen.

She'd been lucky to find such a job, for Antonio and Kenderly were thoroughly selective with the employees they hired. Because of the island's charm and the addictive fantasies it weaved, employees were only allowed to work at the resort for two years. At the end of their service, they were granted a large severance payment and offered another position within Aragon enterprises, headed by Antonio's brother, Miguel.

Her hand trembled as she took another bite of toast. She desperately needed this job and the severance bonus.

Of course, she had to spill drinks on her boss's VIP guest. What was wrong with her? Dario Dicola was a guest, just like any other. Why, then, did she melt into a puddle of lusty goo beneath his smoldering dark chocolate eyes? Heat pooled between her thighs just thinking about his dimpled chin peeking through his five o'clock scruff. His Italian accent had rolled off his tongue—rich and thick like honey. The temperature in the dining room rose by at least ten degrees. She cupped the back of her neck, fanned her flaming cheeks, and crossed and uncrossed her legs, failing to relieve her body's involuntary response to the sexy memory.

The local news flashed on a nearby television, snapping her attention to the reporter talking about the cleanup efforts from the storm. With a heavy heart, Cat shook her head at the devastation left behind. So many people had lost their homes and lives. Most areas still didn't have electricity. Her family was fortunate, having made it through relatively unscathed, with the exception of losing their power for a few hours.

Her gaze was drawn to the time on the lower left-hand corner of the screen. "Dammit." *I'm going to be late.* Quickly, she tossed the napkin onto the plate, ran it back to the kitchen, and thanked the cook for her breakfast. "The mango jam was to die for," she called out over the sound of clanging pots and pans.

A few moments later, she stood outside Kenderly's office, swiping her sweaty palms down her tan cargo shorts. She took a deep breath and let it out slowly, trying to calm her rattled nerves, but her heart raced as she gave the door a few timid taps, secretly hoping Kenderly wasn't in.

"Come in," Kenderly answered.

Cat entered the office. "You wanted to see me?"

"Good morning, Cat." Kenderly looked up from her desk. "Yes. Please sit."

Cat took the chair across from her boss and folded her hands in her lap. She'd rehearsed all morning how she was going to beg for another chance, but once inside Kenderly's office, she was having difficulty just remembering how to breathe. "Kenderly." She sat forward in her seat. "I'm so sorry. It's not like me to be so clumsy. I'll pay for his suit. I'm sure it's expensive, but whatever it takes."

Kenderly held up a staying hand.

Dios, I'm trying too hard.

"I didn't ask you to come here to fire you, darling. In fact, you're taking a vacation."

28

"I'm sorry. What?" It sounded like Kenderly said something about a vacation, but with the ringing in her ears she wasn't sure.

"Cat, you're a mess." Kenderly stood and walked around to sit in the chair beside her. "Antonio and I have been worried about you, darling. You worked through every off week last month and barely took a weekend to check on your family after the storm."

A vacation? "Kenderly, I'd love the extra time to spend with my family, but you know I can't afford to take the time off. I'll get it together. I promise."

"I'm not talking about taking another weekend to spend with your family." Kenderly reached over the chair arm and took her hand. "I'm talking about taking time for yourself."

Cat shook her head. "I don't need—"

"This is nonnegotiable, Cat." Kenderly let go of her hand and returned to her seat behind the desk. "If you love your job as much as we love having you here, then you will take this week off."

A week? Cat knew she should hold her tongue, but a week? "Kenderly I can't afford a week—"

"You can." Kenderly opened a folder in front of her and pulled out a piece of paper. "According to your file, you've accumulated over three weeks paid vacation." She picked up a plastic card and held it out to Cat. "If you agree to take this week for yourself, and only yourself, I'll add a week to it."

Cat narrowed her eyes, studying Kenderly as she reached out and took the Aragon Island credit card, recognizing the tale-tell twinkle in her boss's eyes. What was Kenderly up to?

"Wonderful," Kenderly said with a knowing wink. "I've taken the liberty of having your things moved to the Celestial Cabana at the beach. Charge anything you wish on that card and we'll take care of the rest.

"The Celestial?" That was one of the most palatial cabanas on the island!

"Enjoy it," Kenderly urged. "You've more than earned it, darling."

Cat looked down at the silver card in her hand. No one had ever gone out of their way to do something this nice for her—ever. Saying no would be an insult. *No.* She couldn't. Could she? Maybe Kenderly was right. With her papa terminally ill and medical bills piling up, she'd worked every available shift, and many times doubles. Her brothers helped with the bills when they could, but they had their own families to provide for. Every penny she made went to her family. It would be nice to take a few days to herself. Cat felt adrift in an unknown sea. Even thinking about it felt unnatural.

"Are you sure?" she asked one last time, but Kenderly's arched brow said there was no room for argument. "I don't know what to say."

"Darling, you needn't say a thing. Take the week and relax. As I said, you more than deserve it." Kenderly stood and walked over to Cat, giving her a hug. "Here's the key to the cabana. Now go, indulge," she said with a scheming grin.

Still stunned a half hour later, Cat slid the keycard into the cabana door and opened it to an elaborate oasis.

Surrounded by palm trees and nestled among the mangroves, there were six cabanas on the west side of the island, each secluded and private. In the morning and evening hours, birds sang a variety of tunes, making this part of the resort truly magical. It was Catalina's favorite place.

Many times she'd hiked on the path that snaked beyond the last cabana and deeper into the tropical jungle. Listening to the birds, seeing a variety of brightly-colored orchids, and smelling the salty air were a few of her favorite things about the spot. It was a place of peace and harmony. A place she could recharge between shifts. What would she do with a whole week?

Once inside, she placed her purse on the small kitchen table and continued into the living room, the wall-to-wall sliding glass doors providing a vibrant view of the turquoise water that beckoned her to the white sandy beach. She opened the slider and breathed in the ocean air, feeling a tingle that ran from the top of her head to her toes. *The magic of Aragon Island.*

The view was indeed breathtaking—sun sparkling like diamonds on the water's surface. She closed her eyes, listening to the waves lap against the shore. She understood the magic of the place and how easy it was to lose one's self in a fantasy, for she was doing it right now without an ounce of effort. All she needed now was her prince charming.

A rap at the door shook her from her fantasy just in time. Another second and she'd have been mired in a fantasy with Dario, wrapped in his arms, looking up into his deep chocolate-colored eyes.

"Cat, are you in there?"

She smiled at the familiar voice and opened the door. "Mario!" He strolled past her in a whirlwind leaving behind a cloud of coconut fragrance.

"Wow," he exclaimed, spinning circles as he took in the room. "Take a look at this place. The upgrades Antonio added after the storm really did the trick!"

She chuckled. "The view is still the same, though. That's all that matters."

Mario strolled to the glass door. "Kenderly is really giving you the Cinderella treatment, isn't she?"

"Yeah, she's giving me the rest of the week off. Can you believe it?"

"Oh, honey." He turned around and waved her off. "I know all about it."

Cat folded her arms across her chest and watched as Mario brought in a garment bag and laid it on the bed. "What's that?"

Mario faced her with a devilish grin. "Looks like you're going to the Festival of Fantasies Masquerade ball tonight."

"What?" She didn't have a dress, shoes, or even a mask. And what was she going to do at a ball? She didn't even know how to dance! "I don't have—"

"No time to argue, honey. Your dress is in the bag. Here's your shoes and mask." He handed her another bag.

"Mario, this is all too much."

"Na-ah-ah. Hair, make-up, nails," he said, snapping his fingers in a Z pattern with his dramatic style, "and a wax at six in the salon. You know where it is. Ask for the Mario special." He winked. "And Cinderella time is eight o'clock sharp, or your pumpkin will leave without you."

Cat followed Mario out of the bedroom. "Seriously, why is Kenderly doing this? Moments ago I was sure I'd be searching for a new job, and now this? I don't understand. I don't deserve this, whatever *this* is. No more than you, or Rosa, or anyone else here. Why me? She's never—"

Mario turned on his heels, almost crashing into her. "Honey, Kenderly and Antonio have taken care of each of us when we needed them the most. You know Kenderly adores you, too. She's worried about you. We *all* are."

"I know, but—"

Mario cupped her face. "No buts, honey. Now get to the salon."

Catalina forced a smile. Accepting such a gift would never feel right, but it didn't look as though she had much of a choice.

33

"Oh, I almost forgot." Mario reached into his shirt pocket and pulled out a bottle of perfume. "This is a special gift from Kenderly. One spritz behind each ear, one between the ladies." He cupped his own pecs to form a cleavage line, making her laugh. "And one between those gorgeous thighs, and done. Don't overdo it."

She took the bottle and studied the liquid. *Between my thighs?*

"Just do it, and don't ask any more questions. Tonight is your night to sparkle, my love." Mario gave her a dismissive wave as he sauntered out of the cabana.

Catalina closed the door, walked over to the bed, and unzipped the garment bag. She stood speechless as she stared at the light blue designer dress, exactly her size. She was dreaming. She had to be.

CHAPTER
Four

Beneath the stars at the seaside pavilion, violins softly blended into the lower pitch of the cello, creating beautiful music and setting the mood for the night—magical and romantic. And that was exactly how Catalina felt.

Despite her reservations, she'd donned the powder blue and silver dress, which fit her to perfection, and decided to give this whole vacation thing an honest try. She owed Antonio and Kenderly that much in appreciation for their concern and generosity.

Once dressed, she'd refused to look at herself in the mirror, knowing she'd feel nothing short of ridiculous. But when the soft light from the candlelit canopy reflected off the jewel encrusted bodice of her dress and the long layers of silk and chiffon, she felt like a princess attending her first ball.

A waiter stopped next to her, offering a glass of champagne. She took one, sipping it quickly before she placed the empty glass back onto the tray. Nervous, she adjusted her matching blue and silver butterfly mask and straightened her spine as she crossed the ballroom floor. *You can do this, Cat.* Behind the mask no one knew her identity. She could be whatever she wanted tonight. For the first time since she could remember, she desired to put her worries behind her and indulge, to live a fantasy. She didn't think she could last the week Kenderly had asked of her, but for one night, this night, she could be Cinderella.

"You look ravishing."

"Oh!" Cat flinched at the deep whisper so close to her ear, but before she could pull away, Dario Dicola whisked her into his arms and onto the dance floor.

"Relax," he said, his lips so close his hot breath tickled her ear. "I waited until you put the glass down, so there's nothing to be nervous about."

Cat's stomach flipped and heat tinged her cheeks. "I'm so sorry about that," she rushed to offer again, but when she pulled back to look up at him, he placed a finger over her lips.

"No more apologies," Dario insisted, his gaze so intense, even through his mysterious, black mask, she had to look away. "Tonight, we begin anew. Ow!" Dario stumbled when she stepped on his toe.

Oh, Dios mio! "I don't know how to dance! I'm sor—" At his playful warning glance her next apology derailed. "I shouldn't be here," she said instead, and turned to leave.

Dario refused to let her go.

"Don't go." He gathered her back into his arms. "Dancing is simple, instinctual. I will show you."

He took her hand in his and pulled her close, too close. She drew in a subtle whiff of his cologne. *Not close enough.*

"Relax and feel the way my body moves against yours." He took a step forward, and she took a step back. "Very good." He took another and she moved with him. "See? You are a natural."

"I'm positive I'm not," Cat replied with a squeak. "I'm probably the only Latino I know who doesn't know how to dance."

"Catalina is a beautiful name," Dario purred in response. "Tell me. Did you inherit it from a favorite relative?"

Cat nodded. "My great grandmother. She was the first in my family born in the Americas."

Dario nodded. "From where did your family immigrate originally?"

"Spain, but my great-great grandparents were missionaries in South Africa, so I suppose you could say both."

"It must be exhilarating to have such rich and adventurous blood coursing through your veins."

Cat giggled. "I'm afraid I'm neither rich or adventurous."

"On the contrary," Dario insisted. "It takes a very brave woman to wear such a daring dress."

Dario's hand tightened on her hip before he slid his hand to her lower back, his hold more of a caress than a controlling force as he splayed his warm fingers over her exposed skin.

Cat tensed at the contact, but saw his ploy for what it was. "Does that line work often?"

Dario laughed out loud, the sound rich and unrestrained. "Is it working on you?"

Cat laughed, too. "Not one bit."

"Then it doesn't work often enough," he replied smoothly with a flirty wink.

The easy conversation with Dario served to distract Cat from her nerves and she responded with ease to Dario's every move. Before she knew it, they were floating across the dance floor to the sound of the music. She'd never felt so carefree, the cool ocean breeze kissing her bare skin, her silken dress swishing along her legs like a lover's caress. Her heart pounded. The breathy laugh that escaped her lips as he twirled her around sounded unfamiliar, even to her own ears. She couldn't believe it. She was dancing with Dario Dicola and loving every moment.

"Your eyes sparkle like stars when you smile," Dario hummed in her ear. "Did you know that?"

Focused on the knot in his tie, Cat lifted her gaze to his chin, a very masculine chin jutting out just below two very soft lips that were curled in a seductive smile. A sudden flutter tickled her insides and she made the mistake of meeting his gaze, the intense heat she saw there making her stumble.

"Whoa!"

Cat cursed at her clumsiness as Dario steadied her on her feet, but she'd been having so much fun, she couldn't help but laugh. "I should probably stop before I break something or have to replace your shoes with the suit I've already ruined."

Dario didn't argue this time and escorted her to the outer rim of the pavilion, snagging two glasses of champagne on the way.

"Oh, no thank you," Cat refused when he offered her one. She'd never be able to carry another glass in his presence again.

Dario arched an insistent brow; he wasn't taking no for an answer.

"Okay." She took the glass from his hand. "But stand over there." She motioned to a spot by the marble railing behind them. "I can't spill anything on you from that far away."

When the butterflies finally settled and she had control of the glass in her hands, she joined him.

Breathing in the salty breeze, Cat looked out over the darkened beach. Dario stepped behind her and her body came alive. He gripped the wide railing, trapping her between his arms. His tall frame closed around her as he lowered his head, brushing his lips against the side of her neck. She shivered, fighting the urge to lean back and melt into him.

"Are you cold?" he asked, trailing his fingertips down her arms.

Catalina closed her eyes, surrendering to his touch. "Quite the opposite." The sentiment escaped her lips before she had a chance to stop it. Why was her body betraying her? She didn't want to crave his touch or sigh when she breathed in his scent—sweet like chocolate with a hint of spice.

He inhaled, long and slow, appreciating her scent as he would an exotic flower. "Your perfume... I've never smelled anything like it."

"It was a gift, from Kenderly." Flattered, but overwhelmed by his strong brand of blatant seduction, Cat escaped the confines of his arms and stood beside him against the railing, desperate for something distracting to say. She didn't want to encourage him, but she wasn't ready to say goodnight. "There are so many stars out tonight," she mused. "Emilio would love it." She cringed, biting her lip at the habitual slip. There was no place for Emilio in her conversation with Dario, a near stranger, but their conversation on the dance floor had stirred her longing to hear her son's voice.

"This Emilio, he is your lover? A husband, perhaps?"

Cat grinned. She couldn't help it. Aside from the awkward picture his question inspired, the idea that Dario was in no shy way asking her about her love life, was so foreign, she didn't know how to respond. "Um, not quite. How about you? Where is your family from?" she asked, eager to change the subject.

Dario propped his hip on the railing and took a sip of his champagne. "I'm afraid I don't have the same insight to my heritage as you do yours. It's certainly not as romantic."

"Really?" She knew next to nothing about Dario except that he was an important guest to Antonio, which meant he was no doubt rich and influential in some part of the world.

"I grew up in a fishing village east of Genoa, Italy," Dario continued. Cat furrowed her brows, trying to imagine a mansion in the middle of a fishing village. Dario laughed. "You don't believe me?"

"No, that's not it at all." Cat argued, though she would have guessed he came from old money.

"My parents were very poor, but they did their best, taught me the value in education and hard work. I scrapped my way up and managed to land a job with one of the mafia-owned construction companies when I was a teenager. One of the bosses took me under his wing. Paid for my college and taught me what he knew."

Cat nearly choked on her last sip of champagne. "You're mafia?"

Dario chuckled. "No. They were a small family branch. It all fell apart when the head of the family passed away. I took what I learned and managed to make a good, honest living."

"Oh, I'm sorry you lost your friend."

"It was a long time ago." Dario grinned, but she could see a hint of sadness in his eyes. "A lifetime it seems," he continued with a sigh. "How about you? How did you come to work at a place like this?" he asked, raising his glass to indicate Indulgence's main building towering in the background.

"I don't know, honestly," Cat hesitantly replied. She was sure a man of his wealth could find nothing appealing about a mere hospitality manager at an upscale vacation resort. "I applied out of sheer desperation to stay close to my family. The pay made taking the chance undeniable, and Antonio and Kenderly took a chance on me."

"You have a large family?"

Cat shrugged, cringing inside that she'd managed to give him another reason to ask about her family. "I have two brothers, one older and one younger, and my parents," she added. "I am their only source of income. My older brother helps when he can, but he has a family to support. And my father, he's terribly ill."

"I'm sorry to hear it."

Cat sighed. "It's been…difficult, but my job helps pay for the medicine he needs, so I'm grateful for that."

"Antonio must have seen what I see in you," Dario said, setting his glass on the banister.

"And what would that be?" she asked.

"A brave and loyal treasure, who looks incredibly stunning in blue."

Cat's cheeks warmed at the desire in his eyes and she looked away. "I'm anything but brave." She was just a daughter, mom, and sister, whose family meant everything to her.

"One final dance?" Dario took her drink, setting it on the railing beside his own.

Cat looked down at his hand, thinking at first that she'd better not, but the idea of going back to her cabana alone drove her to accept. She took his hand and allowed him to lead her onto the dance floor.

This time, Dario held her closer, touched her more freely as he led her across the floor in a slow, hypnotic dance. His cologne again saturated her senses, forever searing the scent into her memories. She closed her eyes and imagined what it would be like to make love with him. It had been so long since she'd felt a man's touch. Would he be a greedy, fumbling lover like her ex? She doubted it. He could be commanding, she'd learned, but judging the way he held her, the way he touched her with so much passion, yet so gentle—he'd likely be perfect.

The sound of the cello weaved in and out of the melody as she followed Dario's lead, their bodies flushed from the vigorous rhythm. Pictures of them together raced through her mind. Lost in the electricity between them, she caught Dario's gaze as he slowed to a sway, moving his hands up her sides and over her shoulders.

The music finally stopped, and so did they, neither of them moving away from each other. In that moment, a moment filled with promise and excitement and uncertainty, only they existed. Would he kiss her? Did she want him to? He lowered his head...touching his lips to hers...a slow burning heat flared into an eruption deep inside her.

He kissed her slowly, acquainting her with his touch, grazing her lips with the tip of his tongue until a helpless whimper bubbled up from within her aching chest. She parted her lips, inviting him in, but he took his time, tasting her with slow, curious sips until she was breathless, teetering on her toes, reaching for more.

Dario groaned as he finally plunged his tongue past her lips. One slow, deep thrust after another. He consumed her, obliterating every thought she had except what it would be like to give herself to him.

How good would it feel to have the weight of his broad body atop hers, pressing her into the plush mattress, trapping her beneath him as she cradled him between her thighs, welcoming him into her body? How wonderful it would be to not wake up alone, but lying in his arms naked beneath the luxurious sheets together.

Her fantasy was brought to an abrupt halt with a vision of him sneaking out of her bed in the middle of the night. There was no doubt Dario would be a legendary lover, but any thought he'd still be in her bed come morning was ludicrous. Why would he? He was a rich Italian playboy, no doubt with a long line of glamorous women competing for his attention.

He would have no use for a glorified maid come the end of the week, maybe even the end of the night. He was using her, but she was using him, too, wasn't she? This was her chance of a lifetime to live out an otherwise impossible fantasy.

Cat pulled away, her heart ever stalwart, the driving force in her decisions. "I must go," she said breathlessly, wishing she had the courage to be someone who could throw caution to the wind and indulge in a fantasy, but she wasn't. She was just an average woman who had no room in her life for frivolous dreams. She couldn't afford to lose her heart or her job for a few fleeting moments of passion, even with a man like Dario. Especially with a man like him.

Dario gathered her back into his arms, trailing feather-light kisses along her jaw. "*Ti desidero, tesoro mio,*" his low voice hummed in her ear, the words like warm honey dripping down her spine.

She had no idea what the words meant, but her body responded as if she did. *Dios,* she wanted him. "Come back to my cabana with me," he whispered. "You want this as much as I do. I can feel it."

She hesitated. One night, even an hour in his arms was tempting. All she had to do was surrender.

"Be brave, *tesoro mio.*"

Cat couldn't think, and her body wasn't helping the situation. She shook her head. "I can't." She kissed his cheek and extricated herself from his arms. "Thank you for the dance. It was wonderful."

CHAPTER
Five

Dario stared across the dance floor as Catalina retreated, her shimmery wrap fluttering to the ground behind her as she disappeared into the darkness.

"Catalina, wait!" He weaved through the pairs of guests already dancing to the next set and scooped up the wrap.

He thought to chase after her, but the scent of her perfume on the thin fabric stopped him in his tracks. Easily, he could use the lost token as an excuse to follow her, but he had a feeling any of his usual charming tactics would lead to the same unfulfilling end.

He held the material up to his nose and breathed in her intoxicating scent, already contemplating his next move.

He couldn't quite put his finger on why, but Catalina was different. If he wanted in her bed, and he most certainly did, he would have to play a different kind of game. She was too skittish, but make no mistake, the game was definitely *on*.

The next morning, as the first golden rays of sun flickered along the turquoise horizon, Dario sat in a secluded corner of his balcony sipping his second cup of coffee, emails answered, and the previous day's business affairs completed.

He'd spent the restless night not only haunted by Catalina's scent, the memory of her sweet taste still fresh on his lips, but also by thoughts that stubbornly thwarted his consistent efforts at denial. Without access to his usual meaningless distractions, he was left tossing and turning all night, cursing the singing cicadas. At five o'clock, awakened by the alarming guttural serenade of the island's howler monkeys, he'd eventually given up and hit the resort's impressive gym, using the squash court to beat the loneliness gnawing at his insides back into submission.

He normally wasn't one to lend much energy to nostalgic memories, but the lack of distractions and talk of family the night before had invited them to rent prime space in his head. And they'd apparently decided on a long-term lease. He'd never regretted his impoverished upbringing, but he'd vowed long ago to never live so desolate again. Nothing had ever been more important to him than securing his fortune, but now that he had, lately, he'd been contemplating what would become of his legacy.

Having seen his father's heart shattered with his mother's passing, he'd vowed to never marry. With no heirs, no brothers or sisters or family to call his own, who would inherit his accomplishments, his dreams, and appreciate the empire he'd built?

A sudden ear-splitting screech pierced the air. Jolted from his musings, he looked up to the sky to see a rainbow-colored parrot soar into the jungle canopy beside his cabana.

"*Cazzo!*" He flipped off the tablet he'd been uselessly staring at for the last hour and tossed it onto the patio table. How could he think straight with the constant jungle chatter? He scrubbed his hand over his face in frustration. Why was he thinking about such useless things?

He needed to keep his focus on why he was here and forget about the Latina princess. The resort had its tropical charm and, when he closed this deal with Antonio, it would add billions to his fortune. The quicker he made the deal, the quicker he'd be back home, taking in the soothing sounds of the bustling city, far away from the early morning alarm of screeching monkeys and insects with teeth longer than a blood-sucking vampire's.

Movement on the beach caught his eye and he pushed to his feet, shuffling closer to the patio's edge to get a better view. Catalina appeared, sauntering along the surf. He gripped the railing as she bent down to pick up a shell. A wicked grin spread across his face, a rush of raw masculine desire coursed through his veins as he thought about all the naughty things he wanted to do to her perfectly round ass.

Her sable hair fell down her bare back, hiding the bow tied in the back of her very revealing bikini top. He'd thought she looked ravishing in blue, but the canary yellow against her mocha skin made his fingers twitch with the need to tug on that string and see what was hidden by the flimsy material. He could almost taste the salt on her skin.

He followed the curve of her spine to the sway of her hips as she walked in the sand, biting his lip at the sight of her long, toned legs. The lower half of her swimsuit, while framing her to perfection, was more conservative than he was used to seeing in Europe. Oddly, he liked that about her.

The sounds of the island may be irritating as hell, but the sights were awe-inspiring. Content with the vision before him, he watched her for a while as she waded in the lapping waves, hypnotized by the way the warm breeze flirted with her hair. What was it about her that captivated him so completely, stirring his deepest cravings, yet calming his restless soul? He shook his head and pushed from the railing. Whatever it was, it was time to implement Plan B if he was going to get her in bed tonight.

He pulled his shirt over his head and tossed it into the dirty clothes hamper, pausing when the thought of Catalina being the one to do his laundry crossed his mind. He didn't like it. Not only the idea of her doing such menial tasks, but the fact that he'd given it a thought at all. *She's only a distraction to get you through the week so you can close the deal.*

"Right." *A distraction.*

He changed into a pair of comfortable shorts, leaving his shoes in the closet, and sprinted out the door to the beach.

Not wanting to look too eager, he slowed his pace as if he'd been out for a morning stroll instead of on the prowl. When their eyes met, he smiled and walked over to her.

"Morning, *tesoro mio*."

She returned his smile. "Morning. You're not stalking me, are you?" she asked playfully.

"Maybe." He grinned. "No, I was out taking a walk to clear my head."

Bashfully, she tucked a strand of hair behind her ear. "The beach is a great place to do that."

"What brings you out so early this morning?" he asked, intent on keeping the conversation flowing so he could advance his plan.

"This." She opened her hand, excited to show him several shells she'd found. "They're almost perfect and quite rare to find here."

The excitement in her eyes at such a simple pleasure warmed him deeper than the bright sun shining behind her. "They're beautiful. You should save them. Put them in a jar or something and set them in your window."

"No!" she gasped and dropped the shells back onto the beach, dusting the sand from her fingers. "It's bad luck to keep them in your house."

Dario bent down and picked up the one with the most vibrant colors. "But you said they were rare. Do you not want to keep them?"

Cat shook her head and took the shell from his hand, tossing it back into the ocean. "There will be more

50

tomorrow. These will ride the tides to another beach, so someone else can appreciate their beauty."

He watched as she picked up the other shells and tossed them into the waves, laughing when one skipped across the surface. "Walk with me for a while?" he asked when she was done, nodding down the white sandy beach.

Catalina hesitated a moment, then nodded silently and fell into step beside him.

"I want to apologize for last night," Dario said, keeping his hands tucked deep inside his pockets despite an eager urge to reach for hers. "I don't regret kissing you, not for a moment, but I may have come on a little strong in my efforts to gain your attention."

Cat giggled. "May have?"

Dario grinned. "Maybe."

"A little?"

"Okay, *maybe a little* is a bit of an understatement," he conceded. In her silence, he turned and dipped his head, relieved to find her smiling. "Forgiven?"

Her smile broadened, replacing his relief with an almost smug satisfaction. Phase one of Plan B having gone smoother than he'd anticipated meant it was time to move to phase two. "Good," he said, "then come sailing with me this afternoon. Antonio has a boat and I'd like to see the rest of the island."

"What? I can't—"

"Sure, you can. I taught you how to dance, didn't I? I can teach you how to sail. There's nothing to it, really. I'll do all the work while you enjoy the warm breeze and—"

"It's not that," Cat argued. "Dario, I'm not in a good place for a fling or a fantasy right now. I know you're only trying—"

"To show you how sorry I am," he insisted before she could put words in his mouth. "And to show you that it is okay to relax once in a while. Everyone speaks so highly of you and how hard you've worked to help Antonio and Kenderly."

"You've asked about me?"

"No," he assured her. "Not directly, but I have ears. Come with me," he pleaded again. "It's one afternoon, and I'll keep my hands to myself. I won't kiss your lovely lips again, unless you ask me to."

Cat laughed and the sound went straight to his head. "You aren't afraid I'll accidentally push you overboard?"

"I'm a good swimmer," he said. He turned again, walking backward with each forward step she took. "Inspirational sunset, fine wine, a short trip around a beautiful island. Would you say yes if I tossed in a box of decadent chocolate?"

Cat snorted the cutest laugh. It was working! He could feel it.

"Dark or milk chocolate?" she asked.

"Whichever. Both."

She stopped and turned to look at the ocean. For one brief second, he thought she was going to say no. "Okay, I'll go."

"Yes!" Dario pumped his fist in the air as if his favorite fútbol team had just scored the winning goal. He was acting like a chump, but he didn't care. Once he had her on that boat, she would be all his. All he had to do now was convince Antonio to let him use the boat.

Three hours later, he was standing on the deck of the sailboat, the warm tropical air blowing in his face. Catalina stood at his side as they coasted through the crystal-clear water at the north end of the island, the pristine parcel he hoped to procure from Antonio for the location of his new luxury condos he wanted to build.

"Go to the bow and get ready to toss over the anchor." He pointed to the small hold in the front where the anchor rope was coiled. "Watch the boom."

Catalina ducked beneath the sail, her white tank dress flapping in the breeze around her long legs and hurried to the front of the boat. She lifted the small anchor and looked back at him for further instructions. He turned the boat a little closer to shore and gave her a nod. "Now."

Cat tossed the anchor overboard. He waited for it to hold, then locked the wheel into place and then joined her on the bow, where he retrieved the blanket and picnic basket Kenderly had personally packed for them. Cat took the blanket from him and spread it out.

"This side of the island is so wild and beautiful," she said, looking out over the canopy of trees as he laid out an assortment of fruits and cheeses. "Antonio's efforts to keep the island as natural as possible really makes it special." Dario grimaced and she caught sight of his furrowed brow before he could hide his disappointment. "What? You don't agree?"

He popped the cork on the wine and poured some into a glass, handing it to her before he poured his own. "I don't know." He shrugged casually. He had to tread lightly, but also knew he couldn't lie to her, no matter how badly he wanted her in his bed. "Don't you think it would be profitable for Antonio to add a more permanent residence for those of his guests who wish to stay?"

"Like condos?" she asked with a laugh. "Then Aragon Island would be like all the others, crowded and choked with busy streets and all of its natural resources depleted."

"But what if they were built with care to preserve those qualities, much like Antonio has done with the resort?"

"Are you considering asking Antonio to let you develop Aragon Island?" she asked bluntly.

Dario took a sip of wine and nodded. "It's why I'm here."

"You mean you're not just here to fulfil your grandest fantasies?" she asked with a playful roll of her eyes.

Dario smiled, glancing up at her. "I consider the time we're spending together a bonus."

Cat laughed shyly, blushing as she looked out over the water to the shore. "He'll never do it," she said, her voice laced with more hope than conviction.

"I hope you're wrong," he said, feeling a surprising stab of regret. "The addition of a few condos on this side of the island would bring a considerable amount of stability to the resort and provide a consistent stream of returning guests."

"And add a *considerable amount* to your fortune?"

A string of rebuttals gathered on the tip of Dario's tongue, but he was saved from deploying them by the familiar echo of low, guttural howls.

"Oh, look!" Cat pointed at a cluster of trees where a group of howler monkeys jumped from limb-to-limb. "They're coming out to say hello."

"We've already met," Dario grumbled, but thankful for the reprieve. He shifted on the blanket to sit beside Catalina to watch, his attention easily redirected to the nape of her neck and the short wisps of baby-fine hair that curled at her hairline.

The breeze shifted and he inhaled the brief whiff of the perfume that had driven him to distraction the night before. He watched as she pressed her lips to the rim of the glass and took a sip of the fine wine, remembering how soft they felt. How long could he restrain from kissing her?

"Some things are worth more than money." Cat pointed to the lush jungle in front of them. "The view alone is priceless."

He couldn't agree more. The view was indeed priceless.

"Dario," she admonished when she caught him staring at her. "I'm serious. This part of the island is rich in history. Panama's first people lived here, fishing in the mangrove swamps and coral reefs. They made a living trading fish as far out as Peru and Mexico."

Tearing his eyes from her lips, Dario looked up into the rainforest. There was a sense of peacefulness here. The way the surf collided with the sandy beach and the warm breeze blowing through the treetops. "What ever happened to the early island settlers?"

Cat shrugged her shoulders. "No one really knows. It was like the civilization just disappeared into the jungle, leaving behind only small clues to their way of life."

"I see."

"Some say you can still hear their whispering spirits."

"Can you?" he asked.

Cat smiled. "I can."

"Are you sure it isn't a monkey screaming."

Cat playfully shouldered him in the chest. "You make me laugh."

"I could make you do more than laugh." He pulled her close. Her body tensed as he brushed her hair to the side to get a better view of her neck. "You are a treasure."

Cat looked over her shoulder at him. "And you promised not to kiss me."

He rolled a strand of her soft hair between his fingers. "I intend to keep my promise," he assured her with a grin.

"Are you always this forward with your women?"

Her words unsettled him, but he couldn't understand why. "I like to consider myself ambitious." He trailed his finger down the back of her neck, peppering her with soft kisses. The helpless sigh that rolled from her lips encouraged him to move lower.

"You're breaking your promise," she said.

Dario smiled against her golden skin. Seducing her was fun. He slid the thin strap of her top off her shoulder. "I promised not to kiss your lips," he reminded her, gliding the tip of his tongue along her skin, the wild, salty taste fueling his hunger.

"Dario, I—"

"Shh. Don't think," he whispered in her ear. "Close your eyes." She turned and gave him a protesting glare. "Trust me," he urged and she reluctantly capitulated.

A warm gust blew across the water, whipping her hair. He gathered it in his hand and held it off her neck, nipping the hollow beneath her ear. "Feel the wind on your skin, Catalina. Breathe it inside you," he murmured.

She drew in a long, deep breath and her shoulders rolled forward, the tension slipping from her muscles.

He held her arm out to the side. "Embrace the wildness floating on the breeze." He kissed her shoulder, trailing his lips along the soft flesh of her arm to the tender place inside the bend of her elbow. "Do you feel it?" he asked.

"Yes," she said, her answer heavy with desire.

"Don't hold it captive inside you, Catalina. Let the wildness take you where it wants to go."

She released a dreamy breath and leaned back against him, her lips parted in a sigh. He'd never been so tempted to break a promise. He shifted from behind her, gently urging her back on the blanket, delighting in the feel of her body beside his as he leaned in and kissed the side of her neck. A rush of raw male satisfaction quickened his desire when she threaded her fingers through his hair and pulled him closer.

"More," she said on a gasp, guiding him lower.

He opened his mouth and kissed her breast, flicking his tongue over her nipple through the material of her dress. She arched beneath him with a groan, pressing herself against his mouth. Desperate to see and touch her, he slid his hand beneath the hem of her dress and pushed it up, revealing a sexy, white thong, exposing her plump breasts to the rays of the afternoon sun.

Fuck, she was beautiful. Her skin was flawless, her nipples like chocolate pearls, just waiting to be tasted.

"Oh, *tesoro mio*," he hummed as he lowered his head and kissed one of her pebble-hard nipples, drawing it into his mouth, eliciting another cry. His cock throbbed in response and he flexed his hips, searching out a moment of delicious friction against her body to ease his need.

She tensed, and he moved to the other breast, sucking it between his teeth.

"Dario."

At the sound of his name on her lips he doubled his efforts, determined to hear it again. Her head fell back on another sigh and he grinned, teasing her wet nipple with a puff of cool air. He'd never been this reserved with a woman. He'd never fucked a woman like Catalina, now that he thought about it. He hadn't intended on taking their afternoon tryst this far, and he knew if he didn't slow down, he could risk the chance of ruining his plans for later, but *cazzo* he was losing it. Unable to resist, he slid his hand between her thighs and stole a touch. The heat and wetness of her arousal intensified his need, but she reached down to stop his hand.

"Dario, please."

The uncertainty in her eyes when he looked up and caught her gaze told him she wasn't begging for more this time. Her responses to his touch were so natural, so passionate, he was certain he could persuade her to go further, but he didn't push it. The moment was lost, but there would be another.

"Of course, *tesoro mio*." Resigned, he righted her dress and moved to help her sit up, but not before stealing one last taste of her glowing flesh. "My heart is yours to command," he whispered against her neck as he held himself above her. When he pulled back to look at her, passion had diluted some of the uncertainty in her eyes. It would be so easy to lower himself atop her and take her in his arms, to kiss her the way he wanted to. But he'd given his word and intended to keep it.

"Come." He stood and held out his hand, pulling her to her feet. Instead of letting her go, he turned her around to face the sunset and sidled up behind her. She leaned back against him as he wrapped his arms around her waist, their bodies connecting once again with a perfection he'd felt with no other woman. "Watch with me?" he asked, and looked out at the sun as it dipped below the horizon. "It is a sight I so rarely get to see."

She placed her hands over his and relaxed in his arms. A strange feeling of completeness washed over him, stilling the restlessness inside that had been his constant companion of late. He didn't know what it meant, if anything, but he did know he would never see another sunset and not think of her.

CHAPTER
Six

The mattress dipped beside Cat, jostling her from her nap. Warmth cocooned her from behind before a hand cupped her shoulder and turned her onto her back. She reached up and ran her hands along the bare chest and sculpted flesh hovering above her, not bothering to open her eyes. His scent and touch was unmistakable. No one had ever touched her the way Dario had.

Eyes still closed, she lifted her arms above her head as he peeled off her shirt, arching beneath the pleasure of his hot mouth on her breasts. Her nipples hardened with every masterful flick of his tongue.

"It feels so good," she moaned when he kneed her legs apart, settling himself between her thighs.

Sharp-winged butterflies took flight in her chest as he pressed her deeper into the mattress. It'd been so long since she'd shared her body with anyone. She'd missed this, the basic instinctual need for human contact and pleasure.

She spread her legs wide, yearning to hold him inside her, wanting him to take her to that place where only they existed. Eager and greedy for more, she reached for his firm shaft and guided him inside her, lifting her hips, already throbbing with ecstasy when he drove inside her.

"Tesoro mio," he whispered as he trailed his lips along her neck, kissing her between each breath he took. Every moan, every

pant brought her that much closer to the edge. She didn't understand his mumbled words, but the desperation in his voice brought her that much closer to climax, until the throbbing between her legs spread throughout her body with uncontrollable force.

"*Dario!*"

Cat bolted upright in bed, her chest heaving with her efforts to breathe. Lost in the seductive fog of her dream, she struggled to recognize her surroundings. "My bungalow." She dropped her head into her hands, then kicked the tangle of sheets that had shackled her feet.

For the past two days, she'd been ruthlessly wined and dined, falling deeper into her fantasy with Dario. After their outing on the boat, he'd turned up the charm, offering her long walks on the beach, intimate dinners, and poolside-cocktails as they basked in the hot sun. Learning from his scrupulous negotiation skills, she'd even managed to convince him to agree to hike one of the trails into the jungle yesterday. In return, she'd agreed to a scandalous midnight swim the night before, where he'd wasted no time in divesting her of her swimsuit.

Until that moment, she'd managed to hold on to her resolve not to be seduced by her fantasy, but under the clear starry night, immersed in passion, she'd lost herself in the sensation of their bodies sliding together beneath the warm water. Reality had turned into fantasy so easily, *too* easily. Before she knew it, she'd been writhing in Dario's arms, the plea for him to kiss her ripe on her tongue when a chorus of intoxicated giggles from the beach broke the spell.

Reality had crashed in around her, sending her running from the water. She'd gathered her towel, ignoring Dario's pleas not to go, and sprinted past the cabanas to the private staff quarters. She'd overreacted, she knew, but she just couldn't let this go on. She was falling for him and was certain only heartache waited if she gave herself to him.

Well, that and a dozen or more orgasms.

Cat flopped back onto the mattress with a huff, potent need from her dream still fresh in her veins, making her body crave his touch. She ignored it and closed her eyes, but Dario's handsome face was the only thing she saw. He'd been so kind, enchanting, and romantic, everything she once believed in, everything she wished she could believe in again.

Groaning, she pushed from the bed and made her way into the small bathroom, only just realizing that all her things were back in the cabana. The cabana right next to Dario's.

"Great."

I'm doing the right thing. I know I am. She flipped on the faucet and splashed some water on her face. In two days, he would return to his glamourous life, leaving her behind like the fairytale peasant girl with one glass slipper, a rotting pumpkin carriage, and a broken heart. Thanks, but no thanks. She didn't even know why she wanted anything more from him. It wasn't like she could jet off to Milan with him, even if he asked her to. She could never leave her family behind, her son or her dying father.

A heavy knock at the door startled her. Her heart raced as she rushed to answer it, the thought of Dario on the other side sending an unwanted spontaneous, drug-like high rushing through her veins.

"Cat, if you don't open this door, so help me, sweet baby Jesus, I'll—"

Cat opened the door, greeting Mario with her hand perched on her hip. "What...you'll huff and puff and blow it down."

Mario pushed past her, wearing a sparkling shirt and full of attitude. "Where have you been? I called and called and nothing! You know it's rude to ignore your friends."

"I'm sorry, but I need some *me* time. Please don't take it personally."

"Me time?" he exclaimed. "It looks like a crypt in here." He walked over to the sliding door and yanked open the curtain.

Cat rushed over and pulled it closed again. "What are you doing? He'll know where I am."

"Who? The sun?"

Cat rolled her eyes. "No. Dario."

Shock spread across Mario's face, his voice a few octaves higher when he finally spoke. "You're hiding from Mr. Dicola? Honey, are you ill?"

Cat darted out of reach when he tried to feel her forehead. "I'm perfectly well, thank you."

"He didn't hurt you, did he? Because I'll have to get real." He snapped his fingers and narrowed his eyes. "You know I will."

"Mario, he didn't hurt me." Cat retreated to the couch. "I just don't want to see him."

Mario sat down next to her, piling a handful of pillows in his lap. "Tell me everything, Kitty Cat."

"I can't do this." She huffed. "I can't be something I'm not. He's a billionaire who has everything, wealth, power, and women. What could I possibly bring into the relationship? That is if he even wants one. I just don't have it in me to be a week-long play toy. I can't."

"Honey, you need to give yourself more credit. You're beautiful, smart, and down to earth. You bring him balance. Trust me. I see the way he looks at you. Besides, Kenderly's intuition is never wrong."

Cat shot Mario a suspicious look. "What do you mean?"

"Oh dear, would you look at the time." Mario bolted from the couch, making his way to the door with Cat hot on his heels.

"Let me get this straight. This entire time Kenderly has been playing matchmaker?" Cat exclaimed. "I should have known. The vacation, ball gown, paid expenses, and you—your *Mario spa special*. How could you?"

Mario spun around, pinning her with an irritated glare. "How could I? God forbid if somebody actually cared about you and wanted to see you happy for once." Mario softened his tone. "Kitty Cat, you work so hard for your family, all we wanted was for you to have your fantasy."

Cat shook her head. "You don't understand. There is no room in my life for a fantasy.

"Do you truly believe that?"

"I do," she said with a little more conviction than she really meant.

"Well, I don't. You're just too damn stubborn to see your fantasy is right in front of you waiting to be taken. Dario Dicola is the real deal, honey. Don't blow it."

How dare he? *Stubborn?* Before she could utter her irritated rebuttal, her cellphone vibrated. "Don't move," she scolded Mario. "We're not done here."

Fuming from a cold dose of truth, she strode to her nightstand and snatched up her phone. Her mother's name popped up on the screen and her heart dived into her stomach. "Mama," she answered. "*Dios mio*, Mama! Slow down! You're talking too fast."

Cat stiffened as her mother's words became clear. "Fever? One hundred and four? I'm on my way." She pocketed her phone and raced to the bedroom with Mario following her.

"What's wrong?" he asked in a panicked rush.

"It's my son." She pulled an overnight bag out from under the bed. "He has a high fever. Mama has been trying to bring it down for over three hours. Nothing is working. I have to go."

"Oh, honey, you go and take care of Emilio. Is there anything I can do?"

Cat stuffed a handful of random clothes in the bag and zipped it closed. "Just tell Kenderly I'll call her later and check in." She flung the bag over her shoulder, leaving Mario behind as she raced out the door.

Just in time, she caught the last ferry to the mainland before the crew shut down operations because of the approaching late afternoon storm. Once off the boat, she flagged down a taxi and was finally on the coastal beltway ahead of the evening traffic delays, heading to the historic district where her family lived in Casco Viejo. Anxious, she stared out the passenger window as the rain pelted the glass, praying there were no accidents. She couldn't afford to waste another second. Her son needed her.

The taxi rolled to a stop in front of a colorful, three-story building with an iron railing balcony overflowing with potted flowers. Too rushed to count, Cat handed the taxi driver a wad of bills. "Keep the change."

"*Muchas gracias.* Bless you."

Cat raced up the stairs, careful not to slip on the wet concrete. She swung the door open, throwing her bag and purse on the couch. "Mama!"

Her mother stepped from the kitchen, wiping her hands on a food-stained apron tied around her waist. "*Dios mio,*" she exclaimed, holding her arms out and pulling Cat into a hug.

"Where's Emilio?"

"Catalina, did you get my message?"

Cat stopped before heading down the hallway. "No."

"Emilio isn't sick."

"What?" Her brows creased in confusion. "But you said—"

"I know, I know, *niña*. Emilio was faking. He snuck a hot water bottle under his pillow. I went in to take his temperature. I left for *one* minute to get a glass of water." She huffed under her breath, "*Niño travieso.*"

"Mama, calm down." Cat placed her hands on her mother's shoulders.

"I caught him placing the thermometer under his pillow. I called you, but you didn't answer. I'm sorry to have taken you away from work."

Cat released a sigh of relief. "It's alright, Mama. I'll go have a talk with him."

She gave her mother a warm smile, then made her way down the hallway and creaked opened her son's bedroom door. "Knock—knock." She walked in to find Emilio sitting in the middle of his bed with a long face. Her little man looked so grown up. "*Ay, mi niño travieso.*" She sat down next to him on the bed, pulling him into a comforting hug. God, how she missed him. "Emilio, why did you lie to *Abuela*?"

He shrugged his shoulders. "I don't know."

"I was worried about you."

Emilio pulled away. "You wouldn't be worried about me if you were home more."

Taken aback, Cat looked at him, confused at the sudden outburst. What was going on inside her seven-year-old's mind? "Emilio, you know I have no choice. I have to work."

"But you could take *some* time off. When was the last time you were at one of my fùtbol games?"

Cat shook her head. "This isn't fair."

"No Mama, it's not fair. You're worried about me, well, I'm worried about you. I need my mama." Emilio threw his arms around her, sobbing.

Tears streamed down her face. When *was* the last time she'd gone to his fùtbol game? He'd call her after every game, excitedly telling her how he'd blocked a goal, or made one, but that wasn't enough. When she'd walked into the bedroom, she'd barely recognized him. It seemed he'd grown at least two inches since the last time she'd been home. Every two weeks wasn't enough time with him, and it was breaking his heart.

"Emilio, I love you to the moon and back. I promise I'll be home more from now on."

Emilio looked down into his lap. "Mama?"

"Yes."

"I'm sorry for lying."

Cat swiped the tears from her cheeks. "You're forgiven, my bad boy." She smiled warmly.

Because she'd been so wrapped up in working long hours for the past three weeks, she'd lost track of her priorities to the point of hurting her son. Never again. "Hey, *Abuela* is cooking dinner. Go get washed up."

Emilio jumped off the bed and ran to the bathroom.

She'd made some bad decisions early in life. Like most teenagers, she'd thought she knew everything. Mario was right. She was stubborn. Growing up, she'd seen the love between her parents and wanted that more than anything. She'd ignored her mama's warnings, believing the boy she loved felt the same. When she told him she was pregnant, it was the last time she saw him.

Emilio was her joy, her rock through the hard times. It had always been the two of them against the world. They'd grown up together and she wouldn't change it for all the money in the world. This time, Emilio had saved her from making another big mistake. If he hadn't pulled this stunt, she would have stayed another day in her fantasy.

That's when she decided not to return to Aragon Island until Dario Dicola was on his plane and flying back to his world. She was putting an end to this fantasy nonsense once and for all.

CHAPTER
Seven

Dario cursed. Catalina hadn't answered a single call since he'd discovered her missing from her cabana. Mind reeling, he'd paced all morning, wavering between his inexplicable need to see her and respecting her obvious need for space.

He'd thought he had her. Naked beneath the stars, writhing in his arms, he could almost hear the words on her lips. *Kiss me.* Hell, he was ready to beg *her* to kiss *him* when the other guests had stumbled onto their private beach.

What was wrong with him? This sudden attraction to Catalina was unsettling. A week with her wouldn't be enough. After only spending three days together, he'd grown addicted to her. He missed her smile and the way her laughter lifted the weight from his chest.

Why was she avoiding him? Difficult as it was, he'd kept his promise. But he wasn't accustomed to women giving him the cold shoulder, though she'd been anything but cold the night before. If she'd been any other woman, he would have had her by now.

He reached into his nightstand drawer and pulled out Cat's blue wrap. He sniffed it, loving her soft scent. *Hell!* He couldn't go a day without seeing her.

She'd ignored him long enough. More determined than ever, he cursed under his breath and strode out of his cabana. Someone had to know where she was.

Dario rushed into the lobby of the main building, his attention drawn to the sound of Mario's fingers typing away on the computer at the front desk. Relieved to see Cat's friend, he knew if anyone would know where to find Cat, Mario would. He ran a hand through his hair as he approached the desk, only to be ignored. He cleared his throat and Mario peered up from the screen.

"Can I help you?" Mario asked with more attitude than Dario preferred.

"I'm looking for Catalina. Have you seen her?"

"Yes," he said dryly before turning back to his work with exaggerated strokes of the keys.

Okay. "Could you tell me where I can find her? I have something of hers I need to return." He wasn't lying. He indeed had her blue wrap.

"Like her heart?"

"What?"

"Nothing," Mario snapped. "I'm sorry, Mr. Dicola. It's Indulgences' policy not to share personal information about our guests or staff."

"Oh, come on. You know me. I need to talk to Cat."

"Then call her." Mario stepped out from behind the desk. "Pool side duty awaits."

72

Fuming at the rude dismissal, he swallowed his curse and followed Mario. "Listen, I know you're close with Cat. She's not answering my calls."

"Well, maybe she doesn't want to talk to you. Besides, she's not here."

"What do you mean?" He stepped in front of Mario. "Where is she?"

"She went home." Mario dismissed him with a wave. "That's all I'm telling you."

Dario smirked. "Name your price."

"Excuse me?"

"You heard me. Is it money you want?" Dario pulled his wallet from his pocket. "How about fashion week in Milan, or—"

Mario's eyes lit up. "Fashion week?"

Dario pulled a card with his personal number on it from his wallet and handed it to Mario. "*Sì.* All expenses paid."

Mario's eyes narrowed, his face twisting with indecision before he spoke. "First of all, let's get one thing straight. Cat is my friend and I love her dearly. Secondly, because I know her so well, I know when she's making a huge mistake." Mario paused. "I'll accept your offer. Not because I'm selfish and would sell my soul for tickets to Milan. But because Cat needs this." He snagged the card from Dario's fingers and stuffed it into his pocket. "I just hope she'll still talk to me after this."

Careful not to say or do anything to make Mario change his mind, Dario reigned in his smile.

"I can't believe I'm doing this." Mario shook his head.

Dario whipped out his phone and opened a mapping app, prepared to enter Cat's address.

"Okay," Mario said. "You take the ferry to the mainland port, then grab a taxi and—

"Just give me the address," Dario insisted.

"Hello?" Mario said. "We have rules. I can't just *give* you that information."

Dario rolled his eyes, gritting his teeth against the urge to shake the address from him. "Fine."

"Grab a taxi and get on the Cinta Costera coastal beltway to Casco Viejo. She's a block from the Church of San Jose. Blue, three-story house."

"Thank you." Dario typed everything in, hoping he was spelling it all correctly, then pocketed his phone and grabbed Mario by the shoulders. "Thank you." He nearly kissed the guy before he let him go and raced toward the glass lobby doors.

"Front row!" Mario shouted behind him. "I want front row seats!"

Dario gave him an acknowledging wave on his way down the stairs. He'd get him backstage passes if that's what it took to get to Cat.

Humid air pumped through his lungs as he sprinted through the heart of the resort to the docks, not stopping until he reached the end where the ferry was supposed to be. *I missed it.* Annoyed and out of breath, he searched the area for an alternative.

"Excuse me." He jogged back down the dock to a woman stepping off another boat. "Do you know when the next ferry leaves?"

"I'm sorry, but that was the last one."

Disappointment washed over him, along with another prickly emotion he didn't have time to think about. All he knew was that he didn't want the night to go by without seeing her. He looked out across the vast ocean toward the mainland. Yeah, swimming wasn't an option.

"Are you alright?" the woman asked.

"I desperately needed to be on that boat. I need to get to Cat."

"I'm assuming this Cat is a special woman?"

He nodded, not knowing how else to express what he was feeling. She was special, but it was more than that. He couldn't just let her walk away.

"I normally don't invite strangers on my boat," the woman continued, "but you look as if you need a miracle. My husband and I are sailing to the mainland for a shopping adventure. You're welcome to join us."

Hope filled his heart. "Are you sure? I'll pay. Whatever you want."

"Nonsense." The woman motioned for him to follow her. "We're headed in the same direction. I guess I'm a sucker for true love."

True love? Was it? His feelings for Cat had surpassed a one-night-stand already. But *love?* Surely not.

Whatever his feelings, it was enough to make him do whatever he needed to do to see her again. An hour later, he boarded the *Lucky Ones,* sailing toward Cat.

Once on land, the couple pointed out where to grab a cab. He thanked them profusely and they wished him well.

"Where to?" the taxi driver asked when he climbed inside.

"Casco Viejo."

"Sir, you're in Casco Viejo."

"Right." Dario shook his head and pulled out his phone, flipping to his notes. "Church of San Jose."

The driver nodded.

After navigating through bumper-to-bumper traffic, an hour later, he reached the historic district of Casco Viejo. Dario gazed out his window, taking in the scenery. Block after block of dilapidated or abandoned buildings lined the side streets. Storefronts and shops sat vacant, leaving the neighborhoods a hollowed-out shell. Weathered *for sale* signs were hidden behind overgrown weeds and tagged with graffiti. It was a shame to see such a culturally rich area go to waste.

As they drove deeper into the city, the buildings began to take on another form. Refurbished and painted in bright colors, the houses breathed life back into the neighborhood. A few shops were open. *Probably family-owned*, he thought as he eyed an empty nightclub on the corner.

He could imagine by nightfall the place would be packed with people dancing to loud music. He scrubbed his chin in thought. With his connections, money, and his passion to succeed, there was true potential here.

The taxi rolled to a stop in front of the church and the driver turned to Dario. "Fifty-dollars." He held his hand out with a smirk.

Dario's brows creased. "Fifty? American dollars?"

"*Si*."

Dario calculated the mileage and, by his educated guess, the cab fare should be at most ten dollars. He shook his head, handing the man a fifty-dollar bill. "This is highway robbery."

The taxi driver smiled. "I charge double for traffic delays."

The scent of the earlier rainstorm was strong in the humid air as Dario stepped out of the taxi, letting the thief off. He didn't have time to argue about fifty dollars. He needed to find Cat.

He stood in front of the church, looking east, then west. "A block from San Jose," he repeated the directions Mario had given him, wondering which way to go. East looked more residential. Only half confident in his choice, he strode down the cobblestone road.

A few moments later, he stood at the end of the block in front of a blue house, as described by Mario. His heart raced. He'd finally reached Cat. Every male impulse urged him to storm the gates and claim her.

From the corner of his eye, he saw a woman across the street selling flowers. He didn't want to greet Cat empty handed. In reality, he needed a few minutes to collect his thoughts. Chasing a woman was uncharted territory for him, and as much as he tried to deny it, he *was* chasing her. Bribing her friend, bumming a boat ride from strangers to a town he wouldn't otherwise care about, all went far beyond his usual pursuit of distraction.

He crossed the street and searched the cart for the perfect bouquet when the woman pulled a handful of flowers out. "You look as if you're searching for something extra special."

There's that word again.

Surprised she spoke English, he smiled. "*Sí.*"

"For a special lady?"

Dario grinned, the word *special* growing on him, yet somehow, it still seemed lacking.

"Here." She handed him a bouquet of white orchids. "This is Panama's national flower, the flower of the Holy Spirit. If you look inside the open blooms, you'll see a beautiful white dove. A true sign of miracles."

Dario eyed one of the flowers and she was right. Inside was a white dove with reddish-purple spots on its

78

wings. "This is perfect." He was going to need a miracle to get through his next move, whatever that was.

Dario paid the woman more than the asking price. "Thank you."

He jogged back across the street and knocked on Cat's door. His heart nearly stopped when it opened. Wide-eyed, Cat stood before him wearing a pair of cutoff denim shorts and a white tank top, her hair pulled up in a messy bun.

"*Buongiorno*," he choked out, his voice smoother than it should have been.

"Dario?" she asked, the shock in her voice matching her expression. "Why are you here?"

"You left me no choice. You weren't taking my calls." *And because I needed to see you.* He mentally cursed his lack of courage to admit his thoughts aloud.

"But, how did you find me?"

"Mario." Dario cringed, suddenly feeling guilty for invading her privacy. Intrusive or not, he was here and he *wasn't* leaving.

"I should have known." Cat frowned.

"Please, do not be angry with him, *tesoro mio*." He grinned. "I made him an offer he couldn't refuse."

"*Dios mio*, Catalina." An older woman pushed her way between them. "Don't be rude, invite your friend inside."

"Mama." Cat gave the woman an irritated glare. "I'm sorry, but you can't stay, Dario."

"Catalina, what has gotten into you?" the woman scolded, then offered him her hand. "Hi, I'm Santina, Catalina's mother."

Dario kissed the top of her hand and she blushed. "It's a pleasure to meet you. I see now where Catalina gets her beautiful smile."

"Mama, this is Mr. Dicola," Cat said. Dario bristled at the formal introduction. "We met on the island."

"Come in, come in." Santina pulled him inside. "Will you be staying for dinner? I've made plenty."

"Mama," Cat snapped. "Dario is a very busy man. I'm sure he has better things to do."

"Actually," he interrupted the mother-daughter debate. "I'm starving." He stepped inside, grinning at Cat in victory.

She glared and shut the door.

"Catalina, when you can, come help me in the kitchen," Santina said as she walked back into the kitchen.

"I'll be right there." Catalina rounded on Dario. "What do you think you're doing?"

Expecting her to be more surprised than angry, he pushed aside his wounded pride and pulled her into his arms. While he liked her fiery temper, he had no intention of stoking those flames. Not yet. "I'm being a good guest and accepting an invitation to dinner. Where I come from, you never refuse a homemade meal, especially by your mother."

"She's not *your* mother, and that's not what I meant." Cat pulled away and crossed her arms over her chest. "Why are you here?"

"These are for you." He handed her the bouquet, then leaned in to kiss her cheek. When she pulled away, he released a defeated sigh. "You're right. I'm sorry. I didn't think. I'll go."

"Wait."

Dario paused, glancing down at her staying hand on his arm, then up at her face. "I missed you this morning," he admitted. "The way you left last night...I needed to know you're okay."

"Mama." A dark-haired boy appeared in the hallway. "Who are you?"

Dario peered at the child, whose eyes looked hauntingly familiar.

"This is my son, Emilio. Emilio this is my friend, Dario."

Dario's heart dropped into his stomach. *Her son?*

He remembered her mentioning Emilio, but to be honest, he'd forgotten about it, not wanting to imagine her in the arms of another man. *A son?* A surprising wave of relief rolled through him. Smiling inwardly, he considered himself a fool for feeling jealous over a mere boy. He bent down to the boy's level and shook his hand. "It's a pleasure to meet you."

Emilio looked up at his mother and she nodded. "It's okay," she said, her gaze darting to Dario, her easy smile telling him that she'd missed him, too. "He's a friend."

"Do you like to play fùtbol?" Emilio asked.

"I've never played." He glanced back at Catalina. "I'm probably the only Italian who doesn't know how to play."

"I can teach you," Emilio offered excitedly.

"I don't think that's a good idea," Cat interjected.

"I'd love for you to teach me, Emilio." He winked at Cat. "Hey, can you bounce the ball on your head?"

"Yep, and I'm good at blocking goals. Let's go." Emilio grabbed his hand and pulled him toward the door.

"Cat, will you be joining us?" he asked.

"I need to put the flowers in water and check on Mama first, then I'll be out. Emilio," she warned, "don't go into the street."

"I know," her son called over his shoulder.

CHAPTER
Eight

Catalina filled a vase with water, then arranged the tall-stalked, white orchids, then placed them on the dining room table.

"It was very thoughtful of your friend to bring you such beautiful flowers," her mother said as she rolled out dough for homemade tortillas.

It was thoughtful of him, yet she couldn't stop wondering why he was here. Surely there were other women at the resort willing to have a fantasy with an Italian billionaire. He didn't have to come all the way to the mainland for that. So, why was he here? "Yes, it was very nice of him."

"Why haven't you mentioned this Dario? He seems like a pleasant man."

Ah…yes. There it was, the same conversation she'd had with her mother countless times. *Don't you want a man in your life to grow old with, and have grandbabies of your own? You work too much, Catalina. You need to stop and smell the roses.* Well, how in the hell was she going to water those roses if she didn't work to pay the water bill?

"I just met him." Cat raised a staying hand, warning her mother not to interrupt. "And before you start making wedding plans, he's way out of my league, Mama. We come from very different worlds."

"But he came all this way just to see you. In my time, that meant a boy liked you."

Needing something to take out her frustrations on, Cat grabbed a kitchen knife and began chopping the green peppers her mother had laid out for their meal. "I'm serious, Mama, I need to focus on Emilio. I don't have time for—"

"Love?"

Cat shook her head. She wished that word didn't exist. *No.* That wasn't fair. She loved Emilio and her family, but that was a different kind of love, not the kind that broke hearts and made empty promises with life changing consequences. When her irritated thoughts broke, the silence in the room caught her attention. She looked over her shoulder to see her mother hunched over her rolling pin, wiping tears from her eyes.

"Mama." Cat rushed over and wrapped her arms around her.

"Please, niña', don't give up on love. I don't know what I'll do when your papa—" Her mother paused, losing the battle to hold back her tears.

She'd been so distracted with work Cat hadn't seen it before now, but the strain of her father's illness on the family was more evident than ever. And she'd added to that burden, by leaving Emilio so often. Now that she was home, she didn't know how her mother had kept it all together for so long.

"Papa is strong and he'll make it through this." Cat prayed the words were true. There had been no change in his tumor at his last doctor's visit, which was a good sign. The treatments were working and he'd shown progress, but still the family worried.

"Catalina, you work so hard to support us. It's time you did something for yourself. Live life to its fullest. Don't take one day for granted."

"Mama, I'm fine. You shouldn't worry about me."

"Promise me you'll at least give this man a chance. Don't push him away."

She squeezed her mother tight before letting her go. "I promise."

Her mother wiped her face, regaining her composure. "Go...join them outside. Dinner will be ready in an hour. Oh, I almost forgot. Your brothers will be joining us for dinner."

Cat froze and said a silent prayer. Not that she needed it, but for Dario's sake.

From the living room window, she watched Dario and her son bouncing a soccer ball back and forth with their knees. Dario looked comfortable with Emilio, smiling and laughing together as if they had known each other for years. Cat smiled at the cute way Dario fumbled the ball. This was a side of the Italian businessman she hadn't seen, and frankly, she liked it perhaps a little too much.

Shoving her earlier reservations aside, she opened the front door. "Hey, are you two ready to see how it's really done?"

Dario tossed the ball her way. "Let's see it, hot shot."

The hour flew by. It had been a long time since she'd laughed so hard. Dario was right, he knew nothing about fùtbol and it showed, but he was a good sport. Emilio had taken his job seriously and corrected Dario when the rules weren't being followed. It warmed her heart seeing her son so happy, and if she was honest, she thoroughly enjoyed this playful side of Dario, too.

"Dinner!" her mother called out the front door.

Emilio ran ahead of them and raced up the front stairs.

"Wash your hands!" Cat exclaimed.

Dario put his arm around her as they walked to the house. "He's a good kid."

Stopping before they walked up the steps, she faced him. "Yes, he is." She brushed a piece of grass from his collar. "I think he likes you."

Dario wrapped his arms around her waist and pulled her close. She slid her hands down his chest, feeling the hardness of his muscles and his rapid heartbeat beneath her palms. Their eyes met and her knees weakened beneath his smoldering gaze. The memory of his kisses flirted with her resolve. She lowered her gaze to his lips, craving a reminder of the spark he'd ignited inside her the night of the masquerade ball. It was only a kiss, and all she had to do was ask. *Kiss him.* She glanced back up to see her own plea mirrored in his eyes.

Kiss me.

His chest rose and fell as she leaned closer, their lips so close she could taste his peppermint-scented breath.

"Mama, hurry! I want to sit beside Dario!"

Equal measures of relief and disappointment crashed between them at the sound of Emilio's impatient demand. Dario grinned. "You heard him, let's go."

Cat nodded, her lips still tingling from the promise of the moment as she followed the sexy Italian inside. Panic pricked down her spine as she walked into the dining room. The table was set for ten. She'd completely forgotten that her brothers were joining them. Her family was big, loud, and her brothers lived to embarrass her any chance they got. Dario was in for a big surprise.

In a mad dash, Emilio came running in from the bathroom and started assigning seats, placing himself next to his new friend. Before they sat down, Cat's younger brother, Juan, and his very pregnant wife, Lucia, walked through the front door exchanging a flurry of heated words.

"I told you we would be late if you drove through the park, but you never listen!" Lucia shouted in Spanish as they made their way to the table.

"Catalina," Juan greeted her excitedly as he leaned in and kissed her cheek, ignoring Lucia's reprimand. "I'm so glad you're here."

"It's nice to see you, too." She couldn't remember the last time her family sat down to eat dinner together. They may be loud and obnoxious, but she'd missed this.

Lucia plopped down across the table from where Cat and Dario took their seats.

"I think I'm about to pop," Lucia complained with a huff, her gaze darting to Dario, then back to her as if she hadn't seen him, then back to Dario, her mouth falling open in shock.

"Well, you look beautiful, Lucia," Cat rushed to cut off her expected squeal, giving her a pleading glare. *Please don't make a big deal out of this?*

"Where's Carlito?" Mama asked as she took her seat.

"I'm sure he's on his way. Probably speeding to get here," Cat joked, thankful that Lucia seemed too speechless to cause an embarrassing scene over Dario. "You know how awful taxicab drivers are."

Her brother sat down next to his wife. "See, I told you we weren't going to be the only ones late."

Cat giggled when Lucia narrowed her eyes and pinned Juan with a deadly scowl, but quickly sobered when Juan noticed Dario sitting beside her. *Oh, Dios mio.*

"Mama!" Carlito's voiced boomed through the house before Juan could speak. The front door slammed closed and Juan rushed into the room. "Sorry I'm late."

Cat pushed to her feet to greet her brother, but stopped short when he froze in the doorway, his gaze trained on Dario. She glanced between them, furrowing her brows in confusion. "Do you two know each other?"

she asked as he gave her a quick hug and made his way to his chair.

Carlito shook his head. 'No…no, I don't think so."

"Actually," Dario interrupted. "You're the taxicab driver who charged me triple the cab fare."

"What?" Cat exclaimed, her cheeks heating with embarrassment.

"Yep, fifty bucks from the port to here. Best money I've ever spent." He winked at her.

Cat glared at Carlito as she retook her seat, scolding him in Spanish.

"I'll give the money back." Carlito reached inside his pant pocket.

"No, you keep it," Dario insisted. "You hustled that money fair and square."

Cat shot Dario a glare. "Don't encourage him."

He squeezed her thigh under the table and whispered, "Relax."

"Oh, I like him." Carlito smirked as he reached for his glass.

Once the awkward introductions were over, conversation flowed effortlessly, though most of it centered on Dario. Taking advantage of the rare opportunity, her father drilled Dario on his views of politics, religion, and family. When he asked Dario to explain what he did for a living, Dario hedged a bit, surprising her when he shared his thoughts about the neighborhoods he saw on his way to their house.

"This area is rich in culture," he said with as much passion in his eyes as when he looked at her. "With the right developer, we could breathe new life into the old buildings, bring the soul of Panama back to the people here."

Her father studied him with a critical eye. "You would not build shopping malls and expensive hotels?"

Dario shook his head. "Normally, yes, but not here." He glanced up at Cat, the sincerity in his eyes releasing something inside her. "This place is...special," he continued, turning his attention back to her father.

"Viva Panama!" her father shouted with a laugh. "I think Carlito is right, Catalina! I like him." He began to hum Panama's national anthem.

Cat dropped her fork onto her plate, groaning as she slumped in her seat. "You've done it now."

"Alcanzamos por fin la Victoria! En el campo feliz—"

"Papa, please!" Carlito interrupted and urged him to sit back down. "We know how patriotic you are. There's no need to embarrass us."

"Nonsense." Her father waived Carlito off and turned back to Dario. "What are your intentions with my daughter? Have you bought a ring? Because she—"

"Papa!" Cat coughed. God...what was he going to ask next?

Another hour of *How Many Shades of Red Can We Make Cat Turn?* and dessert was served, and thoroughly enjoyed.

"Mama, I'll help you clean up." Cat stood and began gathering plates.

"I can help, too." Dario took her plate and his.

She froze, arching a brow as she stared at the plates in his hands.

"What?" He leaned over and whispered. "Did I do something wrong? I didn't offend anyone, did I?"

She shook her head. "No, you're doing everything right."

After cleaning up and several bedtime stories, it was close to midnight when Emilio finally nodded off to sleep. She kissed the top of her son's head. "Love you, buddy." She turned on her heels and headed to the rooftop where she'd asked Dario to wait for her.

"*Dios*, I'm glad that is over," she said with a sigh as she walked out onto the rooftop, her private tropical oasis.

Dario was reclined on a dark wicker chaise beneath a canopy of her favorite flowers, his sleeves rolled up to reveal his sinewy forearms stretched out along the back. Time faded as their eyes met. How could she say no to him when he stole her breath with just a single look?

He stood and greeted her. "It wasn't that bad, was it?"

"Like going to the dentist," she managed despite her struggle to breathe.

They shared a lighthearted laugh, relieving some of the tension in her chest.

"Catalina, you have a beautiful family. They care about you."

Cat folded her arms and looked out over the surrounding rooftops, thinking it had been a bad idea to invite him to such a private place. All day he'd been chipping away at the wall she'd put between them. He was so close to breaking through. "Yes, they do."

"What's wrong?"

Cat smiled and turned back to look at him. "I'm that readable, huh?"

"Yet, you're a mystery to me." He rubbed the sudden chill from her arms. "Tell me what's wrong?"

"*We're* wrong." She slipped away and turned back to the sea of rooftops, wishing she didn't have to say what she was about to. "Dario, I work my ass off to help support my family and pay for my father's medical treatments. My brothers help as much as they can, but they have their own bills to pay. I'm not telling you this for sympathy, but to make you understand we come from very different worlds. I can't be something I'm not, and I'm far from the sophisticated, wealthy women you're accustomed to."

"Catalina, I—"

"No, let me finish." She faced him. "Emilio is my world. One man has already left him. I can't allow that to happen again. He's a good boy and doesn't deserve that just because I'm lonely."

"Catalina." The sternness of his tone silenced her. "Answer me one question. When have I ever asked you to be someone you aren't?"

She swallowed her argument. He was right. There hadn't been a single time he'd ever asked her to be someone she wasn't, or even tried to change who she was. He'd known for the start who she was, shown her nothing but kindness, and had awakened a need she'd suppressed for far too long.

She was falling in love with him.

No doubt he didn't feel the same. But she wanted this. She deserved to let go just once, safe in knowing Dario was a good man, someone she could trust with her body, if not her heart. And he would be leaving tomorrow. Tonight was her last chance.

Clutching to a moment of selfish bravery, she closed the small space between them, sliding her hands up his chest and around his neck. "*Bésame*," she whispered, unable to meet his gaze, focusing on his lips instead.

He dipped his head until their foreheads touched. "What does that mean?"

Looking up at him, she smiled, already feeling the bliss of his embrace. "Kiss me."

CHAPTER
Nine

The words he'd longed to hear rolled over Dario like a wave. There was no plan to seduce her as he cupped her face and fused his mouth to hers. The need he'd repressed for so long rushed to the surface, holding them both in its unrelenting grip.

Their tongues tangled together in a dance so familiar it seemed impossible he'd only kissed her once before. Hungry for more, but afraid his rampant desire would push her away again, he retreated, only to be pulled back.

With urgent hands, she pulled his shirt free from his slacks, the feel of her fingertips on his bare flesh like white-hot flames licking at his insides. He was coming undone, and if she didn't stop now…

"Cat," he warned against her lips, but his plea fell on deaf ears.

Her fingers trembled as they played over the buttons on his shirt, one-by-one, until it hung open between them, the humid air feeling cool against his heated skin. Hypnotized, he watched as she pressed a kiss to the center of his chest, his next breath hissing through his teeth at the innocently seductive contact.

"Catalina." Pushed to his limits, he cupped her face, tilting her head back so he could see her eyes, gauging the sincerity of her sudden change of heart. He needed to know if she wanted him as much as he wanted her. What he saw was desire in its rawest form, laced with hope, swirling in her dark eyes, sending a surge of exhilarating power racing through his veins.

Mine.

A helpless squeak bubbled from her chest as he claimed her mouth again, an answering groan ripping through his throat when she claimed him back, meeting him stroke-for-stroke, taste-for-taste. They may be from different worlds, but their hunger for each other was equal. Two souls desperate to connect.

The second his shirt was off, hers followed, breaking their kiss for only a moment. Her bra fluttered to the ground. He reached for the snap on her shorts, popping it open with a flick of his wrist, tugging at the opening until the zipper gave way and the faded denim slid to her ankles. She kicked it away, her hands working feverishly to do the same with his, but he couldn't wait.

He hoisted her up, and she wrapped her legs around his hips. The gravel on the rooftop crunched beneath his shoes as he stumbled to the chaise and lowered himself down onto the cushion, settling her in his lap. Mumbled Italian curses spilled from his lips when she sank down on his hard cock. The pressure was exquisite, his grip tightening on her hips as she shifted against him, but he wanted more. Needed more. He had to see and feast on all of her.

"Slow, *gattina*," he pleaded against her kiss-swollen lips.

She trembled beneath his hands, her desire like the energy of an exploding star, threatening to scorch them both from the inside out. He kissed the bridge of her nose, her cheek, trailing his lips along her jaw, soaking in the feel of her soft skin beneath his fingertips. His groin tightened when he reached the soft swell of her breast.

"Yes." She sighed, tipping her head back, exposing herself to his touch as he cupped her breasts, teasing her nipples between his fingers.

"*Bellissima*," he purred, leaning up to take one between his lips. The heavy night air stilled in his lungs as he rolled the tip of his tongue over the sensitive bud, flicking and tasting, teasing and suckling before he kissed his way across her flesh to the other breast.

Pure pleasure saturated his body when she gripped the sides of his face, threading her fingers through his hair. An appreciative hum strummed over his vocal chords as he opened his mouth and took all he could, everything she offered and demanded.

"Dario, please," she begged, one hand working blindly at the waistband of his trousers, the other held his head captive against her breast. "I need more."

"Me, too, *gattina*." He slipped a hand from her breast, tunneling it beneath her panties. She tensed, sucking in a breath. "Fuck." He groaned as his fingers slipped through her hot, silky arousal.

His head swam with conflicting desires, the need to taste her as strong as his body's demand to bury himself inside her. *Claim her.* Make himself so much a part of her neither of them would ever be the same.

He fisted his hand around the impeding lace and ripped it at the seams, the sight deepening his indecisiveness. Should he lift her over his face and bury his tongue in her wet heat? Or should he just take what he wanted the most, sink his cock deep inside her.

Like the fiery lover he knew she would be, she made the choice for him, grappling with his pants and boxer briefs until his erection sprang free.

"*Toccami*," he urged when she hesitated. "Touch me."

Breathless, she trailed her fingertips over his hard length, the light caress drawing his hips from the cushion. "*Bueno*," he gritted through his teeth, the pleasure of her touch too much and not near enough.

His chest burned from the breath he held and he pushed up and drew her into his arms, unwilling to wait another moment. "Fuck me," he demanded against her lips before devouring her in another drugging kiss. He shoved his hand into his front pocket to retrieve a condom, rolling it on as she rose to her knees.

He watched as she guided herself over him, torn between the need to see her take him inside her, and the vision of her hovering above him like an erotic angel. As she lowered herself, the feel of her tight sheath sliding over his cock, ripped a moan from the pit of his being.

"Ahh," she breathed with a shudder, her mouth falling open as she braced herself against his chest, a fiery blush blooming on her cheeks. "Wait."

"Am I hurting you?" he asked, brushing her hair from her eyes so he could see the truth in them.

"No," she choked out, closing her eyes as she shifted. "It's just been a long time since..."

Relief and more satisfaction than he would have imagined, coursed through his veins. He relaxed against the chaise, loosening his grip. "Take your time, *tesoro*." Grinning like the king her confession made him feel, he traced his fingertip up her arm, over her shoulder, and down to the generous swell of her breast, pressing his palm against her flesh to feel her rapid heartbeat. "We have all night."

***

Cat's breath rushed from her lungs as she adjusted to Dario's size. Swept up in the torrent of emotions she'd long denied herself, she'd forgotten the small amount of pain that came with so much pleasure, but it had been worth it. She might feel differently tomorrow, but right now, in this moment, she felt nothing but bliss.

"That's it, kitten. Let yourself go."

Dario's strong hands kneaded her bare flesh, pulling her deeper into the maelstrom of passion that raged around them. Soaking in the desire in his voice, she closed her eyes and did as he requested, feeling undeniably alive as she let go of everything and just...*felt* him. Her skin tingled with awareness, her body floating on a weightless high. She'd never felt this way before.

Dario's answering moans lifted her higher, and she stretched above him. His fingers tightened on her hips, grounding her, guiding her, his own pleasure evident in his eyes as he watched her and she watched him. The hard ridges of his muscles flexed with her movements, his chest filling with air in sync with her own breaths. Feeling brave and free, she pushed up onto her knees, tightening her inner muscles as she sank back down.

"*Cazzo!*" Dario cursed and bolted up, his arms folding around her, locking her to him as he pushed up beneath her. "You test my stamina, Cat. You make me lose control."

She pulled back to look at him. "Let it go," she repeated his words against his lips.

"Mmm!" He gripped the back of her head, fisting his fingers in her hair, and kissed her hard and deep, releasing the full force of his seductive power.

Their bodies moved as one. Every breath she took was a sweet concoction of sex and passion and…him. She clung to his shoulders as he quickened their pace, holding on as he thrust inside her relentlessly, over and over until the first sign of her climax fluttered around him.

"Yes," Dario panted, clutching her tighter. "I've got you, *tesoro mio*. Fall apart in my arms. Let me have you. All of you."

He did have her. In that moment, he possessed her completely.

"Dario!" Just as he demanded, she crumbled in his arms, her orgasm ripping through her body with visceral force.

A string of Italian words rumbled from Dario's lips as his rhythm faltered. One final thrust and he held himself deep inside her, his head falling back on a shout as he came.

Their bodies trembling, she clung to him as they sat naked in the silent darkness, the only sound, their labored breaths. She followed him down as he lay back on the chaise, resting her head on his chest, listening to the sound of his slowing heartbeat. He trailed his fingers down her back, then back up again, repeating the hypnotic pattern until her eyelids drifted closed.

Ti amo, tesoro mio.

Dario's whispered words floated to her on a dream, a dream she wished she could live forever.

CHAPTER
Ten

The distant sound of children's laughter pulled Dario from his dreams. Normally, the oddity would have alarmed him, but his lips curled into a grin before he even opened his eyes. Memories of the previous night mingled with the feel of Cat's warm body snuggled against him, her unique scent wafting in the pre-dawn air, tempting his other senses awake.

Nose-to-nose, he studied her face, taking note of the tiny freckles he'd not noticed before, and the small lines at the corners of her lips. He would dream of those lips for the rest of his life. Not only of the pleasure they'd given him in the dark of night, but the way they framed her smile when she laughed, or glistened in the sun after she moistened them with her tongue.

He suppressed a groan as another erotic memory of her mouth on him added to his already aroused state. Careful not to wake her, he rolled from her side. Perched on the edge of the chaise, he scrubbed his hands over his face and then reached for his slacks, pulling them on before he retrieved his phone from his pocket and walked to the railing at the edge of the rooftop.

Expecting a long list of emails from his assistant, he opened his text messages instead, his heart pumping faster when he saw Antonio's name at the top of the list. He read the invitation to meet with Antonio before his return to Milan that afternoon, but his excitement was tempered by the sight of Cat sleeping on the chaise, her legs tangled in the quilt she'd procured sometime during the night.

How had so much changed in so little time? She'd completely bewitched him. He hadn't given a thought to his deal with Antonio in the last three days, or any of his other ventures for that matter. It would take him a week to sort through all the unopened emails and calls he'd ignored in his pursuit of her. Nothing and no one had ever managed to distract him so completely.

He turned back to the railing, looking down at the handful of children playing in the street below. A yellow van pulled to a stop at the end of the block. The kids filed aboard, and he wondered if Emilio was among them. He closed his eyes, absorbing the first warm rays of sun as they fell across his face.

What was he doing? Cat had a son, a family who loved and depended on her, the very things he'd spent his life avoiding. He'd built a fulfilling existence without all of the entrapments of love and commitment that he'd seen break his father after his mother's death. If he did the things he was considering and continued down this path with her...

She stirred behind him and he turned to look at her. Still asleep, she burrowed deeper beneath the blanket before settling on her side with her back to him, her long hair spilling over the edge of the cushion. Could he leave? Walk away from her and never look back? It would be the right thing to do for them both, before he crossed a line and could never go back.

When she released a heavy sigh, he stilled, his heart galloping. No matter what he decided, he couldn't do it here. He needed time to think, away from the distraction and chaos her trusting, morning eyes would bring. Before she woke to find him still there, he gathered his shirt and shoes and tiptoed from the rooftop, glancing over his shoulder one final time at the treasure who'd stolen his heart. *His* treasure.

***

When Dario's footsteps faded and the door to the rooftop clicked closed, Cat swiped the tears from her eyes and rolled to face the rising sun. *He's gone.*

He'd left her. She knew he would, and that she'd feel exactly as she did, adrift and hollow, but the lack of regret surprised her. She might regret never saying goodbye, but she'd always look back on their short time together completely guilt-free. She'd had an affair of a lifetime with the most beautiful man. And somewhere in the world, years from now, there would be a handsome Italian who would share her intimate memories, even if they'd not been enough to keep him.

Kenderly was right. She'd deserved her own fantasy, but just as Antonio often warned their guests, fantasies don't always lead to happy endings. They're just fantasies, outward manifestations of hidden inner desires. Somewhere deep down, she'd wanted to be swept away on a warm October wind, kept weightless for a time in the arms of a mysterious island guest. Now the fantasy

103

was over, and for the first time in a long time, she could see through the thick haze of her responsibilities to the things that mattered most. Her son and family needed her. Not just the money she provided through her job at Indulgences, but her.

Wrapped in her grandmother's quilt, Cat gathered her clothes and made her way inside to the shower. Half an hour later, clean and dressed, all remnants of her fantasy gone, she called Kenderly and explained Emilio's prank and her unscheduled leave. She skirted Kenderly's questions about Dario as much as she could, then thanked her for understanding her request to have an extra day with her family. She couldn't go back today, not until Dario had left the island.

The house was still quiet when she walked into the kitchen and began preparing breakfast. As her family stirred to life upstairs, she grabbed a stack of plates and walked to the dining table, stopping short when she spotted the blue tie hanging over the back of one of the chairs. The chair Dario had sat in the evening before, sharing dinner with her family.

She set the stack of plates on the table and walked over to the chair, reaching out to trace the stylish pattern on the fine silk. He'd been wearing that tie the first day they met, when she'd spilled his glass of wine on his sleeve. Everything faded except the memory of that day as she took the tie and lifted it to her lips.

"Catalina?"

The sound of her mother's voice drifted to her. She raised her head, blinking away the tears she thought she was strong enough to deny. "He's gone, Mama."

CHAPTER
Eleven

Dario stood at the head of the conference table inside Indulgences' expansive library. Eyeing the empty chairs, he chose one in the center. The purpose of this meeting had changed, and with it, his need to maintain the upper hand. Finding common ground with Antonio was now more important than ever. A more centralized seating arrangement would better portray their equal footing.

He sat down and retrieved the contract from his briefcase, the scent of Cat's perfume heavy on its pages. Despondent, he searched the leather messenger bag and withdrew the wrap she'd dropped the night of the masquerade ball. Wrapping the fabric around his fist, he walked to the window overlooking the beach, inhaling her exotic scent. Memories of their time on the island and the night with her family, distorted the luxurious view in front of him.

After asking Antonio to postpone their meeting for a day, he'd walked the beach from the resort, all the way to the northernmost end where the thick jungle marked the land he'd spent months trying to purchase. By the time he'd reached it, he'd felt none of the excitement he'd held the day he arrived on the island.

Instead, all he could think about was Cat, the way she looked in her gown at the ball, the way she laughed at her own clumsiness, and the way she talked about the ancient people who once inhabited the island. He would even swear he'd heard the whispering spirits she spoke of on the day he took her sailing.

On the way back, he thought about her family, how much they loved her, and the look in her eyes when she spoke about her son. Admittedly, he'd never met a woman like her. He'd only meant it as an endearment at the time, but she was a genuine treasure, rare and worth more than even he would ever be able to afford. He still didn't know if what he was doing was the right thing, but after an entire night alone, he was sure this was the only path forward. Once he started down it, there would be no going back.

"Good afternoon." Dario turned at the sound of Antonio's greeting. "Sorry to have kept you waiting," he offered. "We were unexpectedly delayed at the airport. Saying goodbye can be difficult at times."

Dario shook Antonio's hand with a nod, careful to steel his reaction to the sudden ache in his chest. "A sentiment I've recently been acquainted with, unfortunately."

"Isn't that Cat's?" Antonio asked, pointing to her wrap in his other hand.

Dario studied it, giving him a regretful look while stuffing it back into his bag and then taking his seat. "I was going to ask you to give it back to her."

"Was?" Antonio asked as he pulled out the chair across from him and sank down into it.

Dario didn't answer, considering the man in front of him. Antonio had been the thorn in his side for months, consistently denying him and his partners even a single second of his time, refusing to hear them out about their interest in developing the island. Now he was sitting across from him, his original intent the farthest thing from his mind.

"How do you do it?" Dario asked him, leaning back in the comfortable leather seat.

The corner of Antonio's lips curled up into a knowing grin as he mirrored Dario's relaxed pose. "To what are you referring?" he asked.

"This whole fantasy island effect," he said, motioning to the view outside. "Is it some secret concoction you put in the drinks? A chemical in the water?" He reached inside his briefcase and retrieved Cat's wrap. "A pheromone perfume you give the guests as they arrive? What?"

Antonio's grin spread.

Dario couldn't contain his incredulous sigh. "Whatever it is, I'll admit it's a hell of a lot more valuable than any piece of land."

Antonio threw his head back and laughed.

Dario bristled at his unexpected reaction. "I'm glad I amuse you."

"Oh, Mr. Dicola." Antonio sobered, but his smile remained. "I assure you, we aren't spiking our guest's drinks or spritzing them with hormones." He rose from his seat and paced to the small cabinet bar in the corner, pouring them both a drink and sitting one in front of Dario before he took the seat beside him. "The magic you speak of belongs to the island, and you are one hundred percent correct about its value."

Dario nodded, taking a sip of his drink to relieve the dryness in his throat. "If what you say is true, it's a priceless commodity."

Antonio peered at him over the rim of his glass as he took a sip, releasing a sigh of approval before he continued. "Now you understand why I will never sell a single grain of sand to you or any other investor."

Dario nodded, still unsure what to believe.

Antonio considered him a moment, making him feel as if the man could somehow see right through him. "Tell me," he finally said, "what plagues you more? The idea that everything that has happened in the last week, all of the choices you've made were somehow not yours? That you were guided by some mysterious unseen force into a fantasy you never asked for? Or the possibility that all you've experienced here was already inside you, a secret fantasy you'd buried so deep you'd forgotten your own desires?"

Dario thought about his question, only to be led to another. Did it truly matter? What was done was done. There was no going back.

"I assure you again, Mr. Dicola. We don't create fantasies here. We only facilitate them." Antonio reached for the contract on the table and flipped through the pages. "This is not the original document your assistant sent me the day you arrived," he remarked before laying it back down.

Dario cleared his throat, more sure than ever he'd made the right decision. "It's a new project. Something...different, special, and I'm hoping you will consider making it a joint venture."

The library door opened and Kenderly walked inside. "Oh, I'm sorry. I thought you'd be done by now."

"Dario?"

Cat's voice brought Dario to his feet. She pushed through the door, and the look of sheer torture on her face propelled him around the table.

"You knew he was in here," Cat said to Kenderly with narrowed eyes.

"Don't." Dario took her hand before she could leave. "Don't be angry with them. I asked her to let me know the second you arrived from the mainland."

"I'll go over your proposal with my brother, Miguel," Antonio said. "I'll let you know something by week's end." Contract in hand, Antonio gave Cat a kiss on her cheek and offered Kenderly his arm. "Let's leave them to talk, shall we?"

Kenderly glanced at Cat with pleading eyes. "Please, hear him out," she said. "It's all I ask."

"Cat, I know you're angry about the way I left, but—"

110

"I'm not angry," she said with a tremor in her voice. "It was the easiest way. I'm...I *was* grateful I didn't have to say goodbye."

"That's just it." Dario closed the door and pulled her deeper into the room. "I know I shouldn't have left the way I did, but I needed time to think and...and plan." He shoved his hand through his hair, torn between his desire to kiss her and the need to make her understand. "I had a meeting with Antonio yesterday—or I was supposed to meet with him—about the development project, but I couldn't focus. I asked him to postpone and took a long walk to clear my head. All I could think about was you, and how much I need you, and then it was so late when I got back. I was going to come to the mainland to talk to you, but the ferry was gone this morning and Kenderly said you were coming back—"

"You need me?" Cat asked. "For what? The project? I don't understand."

"No. Not for the—" Dario released a frustrated breath and took her hands into his own, noticing for the first time just how right they fit together. "None of this is coming out right."

Cat swallowed, looking down at their hands as well, her fingers flexing between his. "It was a fantasy," she said with a shrug. "I understand how this works. You have to go back to your world..." She paused and glanced out the window behind him, her brows furrowing before she dropped her chin and withdrew her hands from his. "And I'm staying here in mine."

A war erupted inside him as she turned for the door. He couldn't just let her go. Not like this. Not ever. He beat her to the door and placed his hand on the knob. "Is that what you want?" he asked. He'd come too far to let her walk away from him without a fight. "Because it's not what I want, Catalina."

She stood with her back to him, her shoulders rising and falling with each of her breaths. He leaned in and pressed his lips to her hair, breathing in her fresh scent. "Something happened this week, Catalina. I don't know if it's this strange island magic you and Antonio speak of, or fate, or something completely arbitrary. But even if meeting you was random," he continued, pulling her hair back to whisper the words into her ear, "falling in love with you was inevitable."

Catalina pressed her forehead against the door, her curtain of long hair concealing her expression.

"Please tell me you feel the same," he said, turning her to face him, stooping down to try to gauge her response.

When he saw the tears pooling in her eyes, his heart leapt back to life, beating furiously. He cupped her face and swiped the tears away with the pads of his thumbs. "Your tears give me hope, *gattina*. Please tell me I'm not the only one."

Catalina shook her head, her smile as bright as the tropical sun. "I fell in love with you, too, but I just couldn't imagine a way for it to be real, for *us* to be real. I still can't."

Dario gathered her in his arms and kissed her, the feel of her lips a pleasure he'd never grow tired of. "This is real, Catalina." He took her face between his hands and pressed his forehead to hers. "Come to Milan with me."

Cat tensed beneath his touch.

"Just for a few days," he assured her, "so that I can gather some of my things. Let me show you my world and then I want to come back here to yours and make it *ours*."

Epilogue

Cat tucked her father into bed. Three hours in the chemotherapy room hooked up to IV bags coursing poison into his veins always took its toll. A year of treatments had weakened him, but knowing his condition had improved more than the doctors had expected, and that this was his last treatment, made her rest easy. Her papa had fought hard and won the battle.

Cat bent down and kissed her father on the forehead. "Mama will be in to check on you soon. I have to meet Dario and Emilio for lunch."

"*Niña.*" He held her hand and squeezed.

"Shh, I know. Save your energy." She knew what he was going to say and didn't need to hear his words of gratitude. The cancer was gone and that's all she needed to know. She reached across the nightstand and grabbed the TV remote, flipping on his favorite midmorning game show. "Do you need anything else?"

Weakly, he shook his head.

"Love you, Papa." She gave him one last kiss before leaving the bedroom.

She walked into the kitchen and grabbed three brown paper bags her mother had filled for lunch. She smiled and shook her head. Her mother's caring nature never ceased to amaze her. "Mama," she called out, "I'm leaving."

She locked the door behind her and jogged down the steps. The construction site was only a couple blocks from her home, so there was no need for a taxi. Besides, her usual ride was now working for Dicola Enterprises as a foreman in charge of the demolition crew.

Dario had made the project a family affair, recruiting both of her brothers to work the construction side of things while Dario, Antonio, and Miguel were the business masterminds. Together, they refurbished old buildings and tore down the ones that were too far gone, bringing a once ghost town back to life for their neighbors. Their passion for country shined through, brick by brick, and in every stroke of paint. Not only were they beautifying the area, they'd provided vibrant and affordable new homes, and were building new storefronts to attract tourists. Dario's vision was coming to life right before her eyes.

As she walked and reflected on the past year, she realized it had been one of adventure, personal growth, and reconnecting with Emilio. Although she missed Aragon Island, Antonio and Kenderly, and all the friends she'd made there, she was satisfied with her decision to stay home and take care of her family. She'd helped her mother care for Papa, went to every one of Emilio's fùtbol games, and immensely enjoyed revisiting the rooftop with Dario every chance she got.

For once, she lived life for herself and couldn't be happier.

She rounded the corner and paused outside the fenced-off construction area. With matching yellow hardhats, Dario knelt next to Emilio pointing up where his uncles stood on a scaffold. She thought her heart would burst with happiness seeing her two favorite guys together. For someone who'd once decided to never share his life or heart, Dario had filled the father and lover roles effortlessly.

"Mama!" Emilio shouted when he saw her, running over to greet her.

"I have lunch." She raised the paper bags and opened the gate.

Her heart fluttered and her mouth went dry as she watched Dario approach. He looked like an Italian god, overseeing the world he was creating. Even on the jobsite he dressed in slacks, a white business shirt, and matching vest. His sleeves were rolled up, showing off his tanned skin. Their eyes met. The same excitement she saw on Emilio's face stared back at her. In one fluid motion, he cupped her face and kissed her as if it had been an eternity since he'd last felt her lips.

"Mama." A little hand tugged on her shirt. "Dario let me swing a hammer."

"Is that so?" She eyed her son, then Dario.

"I made sure he wore his safety glasses." Dario winked.

She wrapped her arms around Dario's waist, pressing her body against his. *Dios, he always smells so good.* "How about you? How's your day going?"

"Mmm, it's perfect now that you're here." He dipped his head and kissed her again. "I have a surprise for you."

She arched her brow. "You do?" She wondered if the stiffness she felt pressed against her stomach was the surprise. If so, the mystery was solved. She already knew he wanted her.

"Come." He nodded toward the sidewalk. "You, too, Emilio."

They walked two blocks down from the construction site. With each step, excitement consumed her. Dario was a master at keeping his surprises a secret. He'd already given her the world. She couldn't imagine what he could possibly be up to now. Whatever it was, the anticipation was killing her!

He stopped in front of a yellow, three-story home with a Spanish-style tiled roof. The smell of fresh paint still hung in the air. A wooden fence, painted the same yellow as the house, surrounded a freshly landscaped yard. She didn't know what it was supposed to be, but Dario's work was as impeccable as always.

"What do you think?" he asked, glancing between her and the house.

"It's beautiful," she said wistfully.

"It's ours," he said, beaming.

Cat's mouth dropped open. Had she heard right? "Ours?"

"*Si*," he said excitedly. "Ours. Yours and mine, and Emilio's. I had it completely refurbished. Emilio has the whole second story to himself." He ruffled her son's hair and grinned down at him.

She didn't know what to say as she stared at the dream Dario was offering her. Her own place? Her first home. Their home. "Dario, I don't know what to say."

He took her hand in his, then Emilio's in his other. "*Tesoro mio*, you and Emilio need your own home. If it's too soon, I'll stay somewhere else. I'm sure Carlito won't mind having a roommate."

She giggled and looked back at the yellow paradise. A promise of a new beginning. Her fantasy becoming her future. "But, what about Milan? Your business is there and your apartment."

"I have enough work here to keep me busy for a while. And there's no reason we can't keep both properties." He pulled her close, the air between them changing from fun to earnest. The depth of what he was saying flickered in his eyes. "I've never been more certain in my life, Catalina. I love you and want forever with you and Emilio."

Time stood still. She felt as though she was floating in a dream. He knelt in front of her. *Oh, Dios.* She dropped the lunch bags, her hands shaking as she covered her mouth to stifle a sob.

"Emilio, come here." Dario reached for her son to come and stand next him. "Do you have the box I gave you?"

Emilio nodded and handed it to Dario.

"Catalina Cortez." He opened the box, revealing a brilliant diamond ring, the likes of which she'd never seen before. "Will you marry me?"

Rendered speechless, she stared at the ring, everything she'd shared with Dario over the last year flashing through her mind. The first time they met, their first kiss, the first time she woke up in his arms after he'd made love to her all night. The moment he introduced her to her papa's new doctors, the surprise birthday party he'd thrown for Emilio, and the trip to Spain he'd surprised her with at Christmas.

All the memories they'd created came rushing back and filled her heart with so much joy. Now he was asking her to marry him? In front of a beautiful home he'd bought and restored just for them? How was this possible? If this was a dream, she prayed she'd never wake.

"Cat, do you need a moment?" Through the blissful haze, she heard the nervous sincerity in his tone but still couldn't believe it. Was he really asking her to marry him?

"Cat, please. You're killing me here."

"Yes," she squeaked out, "I'll marry you!"

He sighed with relief, smiling as he took her trembling hand and slipped the ring onto her finger. Tears rolled down her cheeks as she stared at the ring, a dream she'd been too scared to believe could come true.

He swiped away her tears and brought her gaze back to him. "*Tesoro mio*, I love you. I can't express how happy you've made me."

Cat gave him a jerky nod, still unable to speak. He'd made her happy, too. So much so, she could hardly contain it all.

He laughed as he pulled her into his arms and placed a loving kiss on the top of her head. "Are you ready to go see our home?"

"Yes." She was ready to go wherever their love took them. She yelped when he scooped her up in his arms, sealing the deal with another scorching kiss.

Her son cheered, running circles around them as Dario walked through the gate and up the steps to the front door.

"I see you had help with this little surprise of yours." She tipped her chin to Emilio.

"I played every card I could," Dario teased.

He placed her on her feet as he fished the keys from his pocket. She looked up, taking in their home. She knew whatever awaited her inside would be perfect, but none of it mattered. She had everything she ever wanted standing right next to her. Her heart thumped impatiently as he turned the key. This was it, she was about to step over the threshold to a brand new chapter of a fantasy come true.

A True Love Story Never Ends

About Victoria Zak

Victoria Zak is an international best-selling author of the Scottish Historical Paranormal Romance series the Guardians of Scotland. Her first book Highland Burn, was a 2015 RONE award finalist for best paranormal romance. She has also written in the World of DeWolfe Pack, Amazon Kindle Worlds, for USA Today best-selling author Kathryn Le Veque.

When not conjuring her next story, Victoria enjoys spending time with her husband and two kids.

Victoria loves to hear from her readers. You can connect with her through the links below:

Website: www.victoriazakromance.com

Newsletter: http://bit.ly/1uebjmR

Twitter: @VictoriaZak2

Facebook Page:

https://www.facebook.com/VictoriaZakAuthor

Other Books by Victoria Zak

Guardians of Scotland Series:
Highland Burn
Highland Storm
Highland Fate
Highland Destiny

Daughters of Highland Darkness
Beautiful Darkness
Deadly Darkness
Wicked Darkness

Hell's Cowboys Series
My Immortal Cowboy
Kiss Me Deadly (2017)
Hell on My Heels (2017)

Stand Alones
Once Upon a Winter Solstice
De Wolfe's Honor
The Jewel of Grim Fortress

Other Books by D. L. Roan

The McLendon Family Saga
Survivors' Justice Series
Blindfold Fantasy

Website - www.dlroan.com

Newsletter - http://eepurl.com/bEuTkn

Facebook Page - https://www.facebook.com/dlroan/

DL Roan And Friends on Facebook -
 https://www.facebook.com/groups/DLRoan/

Goodreadshttps://www.goodreads.com/author/show/6
949817.D_L_Roan

Twitter - https://twitter.com/DLRoan

www.ingramcontent.com/pod-product-compliance
Lightning Source LLC
Chambersburg PA
CBHW020409130626
46549CB00006B/2488